Praise for Debbie Macomber's
Bestselling Novels from Ballantine Books

If Not for You

"[An] uplifting and deliciously romantic tale with vibrant characters and a wide range of emotions."
—*RT Book Reviews*

"A heartwarming story of forgiveness and unexpected love." —*Harlequin Junkie*

"A fun, sweet read." —*Publishers Weekly*

A Girl's Guide to Moving On

"Debbie Macomber's finest novel. Betrayal and sorrow can happen in any stage of life, and, in this wonderful story, her very nimble hands weave a spectacular kaleidoscope of courage, struggles, and finally joyous redemption and reinvention. Macomber totally understands the human heart. I absolutely loved it!"
—DOROTHEA BENTON FRANK, *New York Times* bestselling author of *All the Single Ladies*

"Whispers a message of love, hope, and, yes, reinvention to every woman who has ever wondered 'Is that all there is?' I predict every diehard Macomber fan—as well as legions of readers new to the Macomber magic—will be cheering for Leanne and Nichole, and clamoring for more, more, more."
—MARY KAY ANDREWS, *New York Times* bestselling author of *Beach Town, Ladies' Night,* and *Summer Rental*

D0972045

"Tender, real, and full of hope."
—*Heroes and Heartbreakers*

"Once again, Ms. Macomber has woven a charming tale dealing with facing life's hard knocks, begging forgiveness, and gaining self-confidence." —*Reader to Reader*

"Macomber never disappoints me. . . . She always manages to leave me with a warming of the soul and fuzzy feelings that stay for days." —*Fresh Fiction*

"A very heartwarming novel of healing and reconciliation . . . that touches on life's more serious moments and [will leave readers] hoping to revisit these flawed but lovable characters in the future."
—*Book Reviews & More by Kathy*

Rose Harbor

Sweet Tomorrows

"Macomber fans will leave the Rose Harbor Inn with warm memories of healing, hope, and enduring love."
—*Kirkus Reviews*

"Overflowing with the poignancy, sweetness, conflicts and romance for which Debbie Macomber is famous, *Sweet Tomorrows* captivates from beginning to end."
—*Bookreporter*

"Macomber manages to infuse her trademark humor in a more somber story that focuses on love, loss and faith. . . . This one will appeal to those looking for more mature heroines and a good, clean romance."
—*RT Book Reviews*

"There's a reason why Debbie Macomber is a #1 *New York Times* bestselling author and with *Sweet Tomorrows,* we get another dose of women's fiction perfection. . . . In the nooks and crannies of small-town life, we'll find significance, beauty, and love."
—*Heroes and Heartbreakers*

"Fans will enjoy this final installment of the Rose Harbor series as they see Jo Marie's story finally come to an end." —*Library Journal*

Silver Linings

"A heartwarming, feel-good story from beginning to end . . . No one writes stories of love and forgiveness like Macomber." —*RT Book Reviews*

"Macomber's homespun storytelling style makes reading an easy venture. . . . She also tosses in some hidden twists and turns that will delight her many longtime fans."
—*Bookreporter*

"Reading Macomber's novels is like being with good friends, talking and sharing joys and sorrows."
—*New York Journal of Books*

Love Letters

"Macomber's mastery of women's fiction is evident in her latest. . . . [She] breathes life into each plotline, carefully intertwining her characters' stories to ensure that none of them overshadow the others. Yet it is her ability to capture different facets of emotion which will entrance fans and newcomers alike." —*Publishers Weekly*

"Romance and a little mystery abound in this third installment of Macomber's series set at Cedar Cove's Rose Harbor Inn. . . . Readers of Robyn Carr and Sherryl Woods will enjoy Macomber's latest, which will have them flipping pages until the end and eagerly anticipating the next installment."

—*Library Journal* (starred review)

"Uplifting . . . A cliffhanger ending for Jo Marie begs for a swift resolution in the next book." —*Kirkus Reviews*

"Mending a broken heart is not always easy to do, but Macomber succeeds at this beautifully in *Love Letters*. . . . Quite simply, this is a refreshing take on most love stories—there are twists and turns in the plot that keep readers on their toes—and the author shares up slices of realism, allowing her audience to feel right at home as they follow a cast of familiar characters living in the small coastal town of Cedar Cove, where life is interesting, to say the least." —*Bookreporter*

"*Love Letters* is another wonderful story in the Rose Harbor series. Genuine life struggles with heartwarming endings for the three couples in this book make it special. Readers won't be able to get enough of Macomber's gentle storytelling. Fans already know what a charming place Rose Harbor is and new readers will love discovering it as well." —*RT Book Reviews* (4½ stars)

Rose Harbor in Bloom

"[Debbie] Macomber uses warmth, humor and superb storytelling skills to deliver a tale that charms and entertains." —*BookPage*

"A wonderful reading experience . . . As [the characters'] stories unfold, you almost feel they have become friends."

—Wichita Falls *Times Record News*

"No one tugs at readers' heartstrings quite as effectively as Macomber." —*Chicago Tribune*

"The characters and their various entanglements are sure to resonate with Macomber fans. . . . The book sets up an appealing milieu of townspeople and visitors that sets the stage for what will doubtless be many further adventures at the Inn at Rose Harbor." —*The Seattle Times*

"Debbie Macomber is the reigning queen of women's fiction." —*The Sacramento Bee*

"Debbie Macomber has written a charming, cathartic romance full of tasteful passion and good sense. Reading it is a lot like enjoying comfort food, as you know the book will end well and leave you feeling pleasant and content. The tone is warm and serene, and the characters are likeable yet realistic. . . . *The Inn at Rose Harbor* is a wonderful novel that will keep the reader's undivided attention." —*Bookreporter*

"Macomber has outdone herself . . . with this heart-warming new series and the charming characters at *The Inn at Rose Harbor*. . . . A wonderful tale of healing and peace." —*The Free Lance–Star*

"*The Inn at Rose Harbor* is a comforting book, one that will welcome readers just as Jo Marie and her inn welcome guests." —*Vibrant Nation*

"A warm and cosy read that tugs at the heartstrings, with love and redemption blooming when it is least expected."
—*The Toowoomba Chronicle* (Australia)

"The prolific Macomber introduces a spin-off of sorts from her popular Cedar Cove series, still set in that fictional small town but centered on Jo Marie Rose, a youngish widow who buys and operates the bed and breakfast of the title. This clever premise allows Macomber to craft stories around the B&B's guests, Abby and Josh in this inaugural effort, while using Jo Marie and her ongoing recovery from the death of her husband Paul in Afghanistan as the series' anchor. . . . With her characteristic optimism, Macomber provides fresh starts for both." —*Booklist*

"Emotionally charged romance." —*Kirkus Reviews*

Blossom Street

Blossom Street Brides

"[An] enjoyable read that pulls you right in from page one." —*Fresh Fiction*

"A master at writing stories that embrace both romance and friendship, [Debbie] Macomber can always be counted on for an enjoyable page-turner, and this Blossom Street installment is no exception." —*RT Book Reviews*

"A wonderful, love-affirming novel . . . an engaging, emotionally fulfilling story that clearly shows why [Macomber] is a peerless storyteller." —*Examiner.com*

"Rewarding . . . Macomber amply delivers her signature engrossing relationship tales, wrapping her readers in warmth as fuzzy and soft as a hand-knitted creation from everyone's favorite yarn shop." —*Bookreporter*

"Fans will happily return to the warm, welcoming sanctuary of Macomber's Blossom Street, catching up with old friends from past Blossom Street books and meeting new ones being welcomed into the fold." —*Kirkus Reviews*

"Macomber's nondenominational-inspirational women's novel, with its large cast of characters, will resonate with fans of the popular series." —*Booklist*

"*Blossom Street Brides* gives Macomber fans sympathetic characters who strive to make the right choices as they cope with issues that face many of today's women. Readers will thoroughly enjoy spending time on Blossom Street once again and watching as Lydia, Bethanne and Lauren struggle to solve their problems, deal with family crises, fall in love and reach their own happy endings."
—*BookPage*

Starting Now

"Macomber has a masterful gift of creating tales that are both mesmerizing and inspiring, and her talent is at its peak with *Starting Now*. Her Blossom Street characters seem as warm and caring as beloved friends, and the new characters ease into the series smoothly. The storyline moves along at a lovely pace, and it is a joy to sit down and savor the world of Blossom Street once again."
—Wichita Falls *Times Record News*

"Macomber understands the often complex nature of a woman's friendships, as well as the emotional language women use with their friends."
—*New York Journal of Books*

"There is a reason that legions of Macomber fans ask for more Blossom Street books. They fully engage her readers as her characters discover happiness, purpose, and meaning in life. . . . Macomber's feel-good novel, emphasizing interpersonal relationships and putting people above status and objects, is truly satisfying."
—*Booklist* (starred review)

"Macomber's writing and storytelling deliver what she's famous for—a smooth, satisfying tale with characters her fans will cheer for and an arc that is cozy, heartwarming and ends with the expected happily-ever-after."
—*Kirkus Reviews*

"Macomber's many fans are going to be over the moon with her latest Blossom Street novel. *Starting Now* combines Macomber's winning elements of romance and friendship, along with a search for one woman's life's meaning—all cozily bundled into a warmly satisfying story that is the very definition of 'comfort reading.'"
—*Bookreporter*

"Macomber's latest Blossom Street novel is a sweet story that tugs on the heartstrings and hits on the joy of family, friends and knitting, as readers have come to expect."
—*RT Book Reviews* (4½ stars)

"The return to Blossom Street is an engaging visit for longtime readers as old friends play secondary roles while newcomers take the lead. . . . Fans will enjoy the mixing of friends and knitting with many kinds of loving relationships." —*Genre Go Round Reviews*

Christmas Novels

Twelve Days of Christmas

"Another heartwarming seasonal Macomber tale, which fans will find as bright and cozy as a blazing fire on Christmas Eve." —*Kirkus Reviews*

"*Twelve Days of Christmas* is a delightful, charming read for anyone looking for an enjoyable Christmas novel. . . . Settle in with a warm blanket and a cup of hot chocolate, and curl up for some Christmas fun with Debbie Macomber's latest festive read." —*Bookreporter*

"If you're looking for a quick but meaningful holiday romance that will be sure to spark a need inside you to show others kindness, look no further than *Twelve Days of Christmas*." —*Harlequin Junkie*

"*Twelve Days of Christmas* is a charming, heartwarming holiday tale. With poignant characters and an enchanting plot, Macomber again burrows into the fragility of human emotions to arrive at a delightful conclusion."
—*New York Journal of Books*

Dashing Through the Snow

"Wonderful and heartwarming . . . full of fun, laughter, and love." —*Romance Reviews Today*

"This Christmas romance from Macomber is both sweet and sincere." —*Library Journal*

"There's just the right amount of holiday cheer. . . . This road-trip romance is full of high jinks and the kooky characters Macomber does so well."
—*RT Book Reviews*

Mr. Miracle

"Macomber's Christmas novels are always something to cherish. *Mr. Miracle* is a sweet and innocent story that will lift your spirits during the holidays and throughout the year. Celebrating the comforts of home, family traditions, forgiveness and love, this is the perfect, quick Christmas read." —*RT Book Reviews*

"[Macomber] writes about romance, family and friendship with a gentle, humorous touch."
　　　　　　—*Tampa Bay Times*

"Macomber spins another sweet, warmhearted holiday tale that will be as comforting to her fans as hot chocolate on Christmas morning." —*Kirkus Reviews*

"This gentle, inspiring romance will be a sought-after read." —*Library Journal*

"Macomber cheerfully presents a holiday story that combines the winsomeness of a visiting angel (similar to Clarence from *It's a Wonderful Life*) with the more poignant soulfulness of *A Christmas Carol* to bring to life a memorable reading experience." —*Bookreporter*

"Macomber's name is almost as closely linked to Christmas reading as that of Charles Dickens. . . . [*Mr. Miracle*] has enough sweetness, charm, and seasonal sentiment to make Macomber fans happy." —*The Romance Dish*

Starry Night

"Contemporary romance queen Macomber hits the sweet spot with this tender tale of impractical love. . . . A delicious Christmas miracle well worth waiting for."
　　　　　　—*Publishers Weekly* (starred review)

"[A] holiday confection . . . as much a part of the season for some readers as cookies and candy canes."
—*Kirkus Reviews*

"A sweet contemporary Christmas romance . . . [that] the best-selling author's many fans will enjoy."
—*Library Journal*

"Macomber can be depended on for an excellent story. . . . Readers will remain firmly planted in the beginnings of a beautiful love story between two of the most unlikely characters." —*RT Book Reviews* (Top Pick, 4½ stars)

"Macomber, the prolific and beloved author of countless bestsellers, has penned a romantic story that will pull at your heartstrings with its holiday theme and emphasis on love and finding that special someone."
—*Bookreporter*

"Magical . . . Macomber has given us another delightful romantic story to cherish. This one will touch your heart just as much as her other Christmas stories. Don't miss it!" —*Fresh Fiction*

Angels at the Table

"This delightful mix of romance, humor, hope and happenstance is the perfect recipe for holiday cheer."
—*Examiner.com*

"Rings in Christmas in tried-and-true Macomber style, with romance and a touch of heavenly magic."
—*Kirkus Reviews*

"The angels' antics are a hugely hilarious and entertaining bonus to a warm love story."—*Bookreporter*

"[A] sweetly charming holiday romance."
—*Library Journal*

Christmas 2016

Dear Friends,

On a recent Christmas shopping trip when the mall was packed and there was barely a parking space to be had, a woman cheated me out of a spot. I won't go into the details of how she did this; suffice to say it was low-down and dirty. I'm sure something like this has probably happened to all of us. And if you're like me, your thoughts were not of a Christian nature. I took a deep breath, said a prayer, and moved on, grumbling under my breath and thinking how unkind that woman was. And at Christmastime! What the world needed, I decided, was a shot of kindness.

Kindness is the plot premise of this book. My heroine butts heads with someone she decides needs a shot of kindness in his life and so she takes on the challenge of twelve days of kindness with surprising results.

The dedication to this book goes to a dear, dear high school friend who died a couple years back. Cindy bought every book I ever wrote. I saw her only once after we graduated, when I surprised her and arrived at her daughter's wedding with two other of our high school friends. Her heart was warm and generous. Her love and support meant the world to me.

You, my readers, have guided my writing career from my first published book until this very day. I read every letter and every note sent via my webpage. Thank you for your input through the years. Don't stop now. You can reach me through my website, debbiemacomber.com, or on Facebook or Twitter. If you'd rather write, my mailing address is P.O. Box 1458, Port Orchard, WA 98366.

My hope is that this book will put you in the Christmas spirit, and if some unkind person steals your parking spot at the mall, be kind, even if you have to do it with gritted teeth.

Merry Christmas,

Debbie Macomber

DEBBIE MACOMBER

Twelve Days of Christmas

A Novel

BALLANTINE BOOKS · NEW YORK

2017 Ballantine Books Mass Market Edition

Copyright © 2016 by Debbie Macomber
Excerpt from *Merry and Bright* by Debbie Macomber copyright © 2017 by Debbie Macomber

Published in the United States by Ballantine Books, an imprint of Random House, a division of Penguin Random House LLC, New York.

BALLANTINE and the HOUSE colophon are registered trademarks of Penguin Random House LLC.

Originally published in hardcover in the United States by Ballantine Books, an imprint of Random House, a division of Penguin Random House LLC, in 2016.

This book contains an excerpt from the forthcoming book *Merry and Bright* by Debbie Macomber. This excerpt has been set for this edition only and may not reflect the final content of the forthcoming edition.

ISBN 978-0-553-39175-6

Ebook ISBN 978-0-553-39174-9

Cover design: Lynn Andreozzi
Cover illustration: Alan Ayers

Printed in the United States of America

randomhousebooks.com

9 8 7 6 5 4 3 2 1

Ballantine Books mass market edition: November 2017

In memory of
Cindy Thoma DeBerry,
with love to her husband
and children

Chapter One

Cain Maddox stepped into the elevator, and then just as the doors were about to close he heard a woman call out.

"Hold that for me."

Cain thrust out his arm to keep the doors from sliding shut. He inwardly groaned when he saw the woman who lived across the hall come racing toward him. He kept his eyes trained straight ahead, not inviting conversation. He'd run into this particular woman several times in the last few months since he'd moved into the building. She'd stopped several times to pet Schroeder, his Irish setter. The one he'd inherited from his grandfather when Bernie had moved into the assisted-living complex. She'd chattered away, lavishing affection on the dog. Not the talkative type, Cain responded minimally to her questions. He liked her all right, but she was a bit much, over the top with that cutesy smile. Okay, he'd admit it. He found her attractive. He wasn't sure what it was about her, because usually the chirpy, happy ones didn't appeal to him. Regardless, nothing would come of it and that suited him. He knew better. Yet every time he saw her a yellow light started flashing in his head. *Warning, warning. Danger ahead.* Cain could feel this woman was trouble the first moment he saw her and heard her exuberant "good morning." Even her name was cheerful: Julia. Looking at her, it was easy to envision the opening scene from *The Sound of Music,* with Julie Andrews twirling around, arms extended, singing, joyful, excited. Even the thought was enough to make Cain cringe. He could do happy, just not first thing in the morning.

To put it simply, he found little good about mornings, and second, he'd learned a long time ago not to trust women, especially the types who were enthusiastic and friendly. Experience had taught him well, and having been burned once, he wasn't eager to repeat the experience.

"Thanks," she said a bit breathlessly as she floated into the elevator. Yes, floated. Her coat swirled around her as she came to stand beside him. On her coat's lapel she wore a pretty Christmas tree pin that sparkled with jewel-tone stones. "I'm running late this morning."

Pushing the button to close the door, Cain ignored her. He didn't mean to be rude, but he wasn't up for conversation.

"Didn't I see you walking Schroeder in the dog park the other day?" she asked.

"No." He hadn't seen her. Maybe he had, but he wasn't willing to admit it.

"Really? I'm pretty sure I saw you."

He let her comment fall into empty space. Could this elevator move any slower?

Fortunately, the elevator arrived at the foyer before she could continue the conversation.

"You aren't much of a morning person, are you?" she asked as he collected his newspaper, tucked it under his arm, and headed for the door.

Julia reached for her own and followed him. Would he never shake this woman? They were welcomed by the Seattle drizzle that was part of the winter norm for the Pacific Northwest. Cain's office at the insurance company where he worked as an actuary was within easy walking distance. Julia matched her steps with his until she reached the bus stop outside the Starbucks, where, thankfully, she stopped.

"Have a good day," she called after him.

Cain would, especially now that he was free of Ms. Sunshine.

"Excuse me?" Julia Padden stood in the foyer of her apartment building the following morning, astonished that her neighbor would steal her newspaper while she stood directly in front of him. She braced her fist against her hip and raised both her finely shaped eyebrows at him.

Showing his displeasure, Cain Maddox turned to face her, newspaper in hand. He had to be the most unpleasant human being she'd ever met. She'd tried the friendly route and got the message. Even his dog had better manners than he did.

"I believe that newspaper is mine." Her apartment number had been clearly written with a bold Sharpie over the plastic wrapper. This was no innocent mistake. For whatever reason, Cain had taken a disliking to her. Well, fine, she could deal with that, but she wasn't about to let him walk all over her and she wasn't going to stand idly by and let him steal from her, either.

At the sound of her voice, Cain looked up.

Irritated and more than a little annoyed, Julia thrust out her hand, palm up. "My newspaper, please."

To her astonishment, he hesitated. Oh puleese!! She'd caught him red-handed in the act and he had the nerve to look irritated *at her.* How typical. Not only was he reluctant to return it, but he didn't have the common decency to look the least bit guilty. She'd say one thing about him . . . the man had nerve.

"Someone took mine," he explained, as if that gave him the right to steal hers. "Take someone else's. It doesn't matter if it's technically yours or not."

"It most certainly does; it matters to me." To prove her point, she jerked her hand at him a second time. "I am not taking someone else's newspaper and you most certainly aren't taking mine; now give it to me."

"Okay, fine." He slapped the newspaper into her open palm, then reached over and snagged some other unsuspecting apartment owner's.

Julia's jaw sagged open. "I can't believe you did that."

He rolled his eyes, tucked the newspaper under his arm, and headed toward the revolving door, briefcase in hand.

This wasn't the first time her morning paper had mysteriously disappeared, either, and now she knew who was responsible. Not only was Cain Maddox unfriendly, he was a thief. Briefly she wondered what else he might be responsible for taking. And this close to Christmas, too, the season of goodwill and charity. Of course theft was wrong at any time of the year, but resorting to it during the holidays made it downright immoral. Apparently, her grumpy neighbor hadn't taken the spirit of Christmas to heart.

That shouldn't surprise her.

Cain and Julia often left for work close to the same time in the morning. Three times this week they'd inadvertently met at the elevator. Being a morning person and naturally cheerful, Julia always greeted him with a sunny smile and a warm "good morning." The most response she'd gotten out of him was a terse nod. Mostly he ignored her, as if he hadn't heard her speak.

Julia waited until she was on the bus before she called her best friend, Cammie Nightingale, who now lived outside of Denver. They'd attended college together. Cammie had graduated ahead of her when Julia's finances had dried up and she'd been forced to take night classes and work full-time. After seeing so many of her friends struggling to pay off student loans, Julia had opted to avoid the financial struggles. Yes, it took her longer to get her degree in communications, and no, she hadn't found the job of her dreams, but she was close, so close. Furthermore, she was debt-free. Currently she worked at Macy's department store, where she'd been employed for the last seven years.

"You won't believe what happened this morning," she said as soon as Cammie picked up. Her friend was married and had a two-year-old and a newborn.

"Hold on a minute," Cammie said.

In her irritation, Julia hadn't asked if Cammie could talk. She waited a couple minutes before her friend picked up again.

"What's going on?"

"My disagreeable neighbor, the one I told you about, is a thief. He tried to steal my newspaper."

"He didn't?"

"I caught him red-handed, and when I confronted him and demanded he give it back he took someone else's."

"What? You're kidding me."

"No joke. Not only that, he was rude *again*." Come to think of it, he'd never been anything but unfriendly. It was men like him who put a damper on Christmas. Julia refused to let him or anyone else spoil her holidays.

"Are you talking about the guy who lives across the hall from you?"

"The very one." The more Julia thought about what he'd done, the more upset she got. Okay, so he wasn't a morning person. She could deal with that. But to steal her newspaper? That was low.

"What do you know about him?" Cammie asked.

"Nothing . . . well, other than he has a gorgeous Irish setter that he walks every morning." She'd tried being neighborly, but Cain had let it be known he wasn't interested. She'd started more than one conversation only to be subtly and not so subtly informed he took exception to small talk. After several such attempts, she got the message.

"Maybe he's shy."

Cammie possessed a generous spirit, but this time she was wrong. Anyone who'd take her newspaper without a shred of guilt wasn't shy. "I doubt it. Trust me on this. Cain Maddox isn't shy, and furthermore, he's not to be trusted."

"You don't know that."

"You're wrong. I have this gift, a sixth sense about men. This one is sinister."

Cammie's laughter filled the phone. "Sinister? Come on, Julia."

"I'm serious," she insisted. "Just what kind of man steals a newspaper? I don't know what I ever did to offend him, but he's made it more than clear he would rather kiss a snake than have anything to do with me." That bothered Julia more than she was comfortable admitting. He was kinda cute, too, in a stiff sort of way. He was tall, a good six or seven inches above her own five-foot-five frame.

His hair was dark and cut in a way that said he was a professional. The shape of his jaw indicated he had a stubborn bent, but that could be conjecture on her part, based on what she knew about him. And as best she could tell, he didn't possess a single laugh line, although he did have beautiful, clear dark chocolate eyes.

The only time she'd seen him in anything but a suit was

when he was at the dog park. He wore a jacket with the name of an insurance company and logo, which she assumed he was connected to in some way, and jeans. Even then he didn't look relaxed, and he held himself away from others.

"Are you attracted to him?" Cammie asked.

"You've got to be kidding me. No way!"

"I have a feeling this is why you're thirty-one and not in a serious relationship. How long are you going to hold on to Dylan, Julia?"

"That again?" Julia didn't have time for relationships and she for sure wasn't going to drag Dylan into the conversation. She was over him and had been for a long time. The problem was she had no time to date, between working and volunteering at church and for the Boys and Girls Club. Cammie knew that.

Besides, she had more important matters on her mind.

The blog. The challenge.

She'd gone through two intense interviews at Harvestware, a major software company, and the list had been narrowed down to two people. Because the job was in social media, the company had suggested a competition between the two candidates in the form of a blog. The one who could generate the largest following in the month of December would be awarded the job.

Julia had gladly accepted the challenge. Unfortunately, she hadn't had a lot of success so far; her following was minimal at best. This was her chance to prove herself.

"Maybe your neighbor is the man of your dreams."

"Cain Maddox? He's cold, Cammie. You haven't seen

him. I have. Trust me—he's not the kind of man you'd want to meet in a dark alley."

The more Julia thought about it, the more convinced she became that her neighbor was some disreputable character. A chill went down her spine just thinking about the cold look in his eyes.

Cammie laughed out loud. "Your creative imagination is getting away from you, my friend."

"Maybe, but I doubt it."

"Julia," her friend said in that calm way of hers that suggested Julia was overreacting. "He took your newspaper; he didn't threaten to bury you in concrete."

"It's the look in his eyes, like he sees straight through people."

"You've noticed his eyes?"

"Yes, they're brown and dark. Real dark and distant." Okay, Cammie was probably right. To see him in criminal terms was a bit of a stretch, but Julia wasn't exactly having warm, cozy feelings toward her neighbor.

"If that's the case, then I think you should kill him," Cammie suggested.

Julia gasped. She couldn't believe her bestie would even hint at such a thing.

"Kill him with kindness," Cammie elaborated.

"This guy needs a whole lot more than kindness." Leave it to her tenderhearted friend to suggest something sweet and good.

"It's twelve days until Christmas," she added after a moment, sounding excited.

"Yes. So?"

"This is it, Julia. You've been wanting an idea that would generate interest in your blog. Your neighbor is the perfect subject." Cammie seemed to be growing more enthused by the second. "Weren't you saying just the other day how you were desperate for an over-the-top idea?"

"Well, yes, but . . ."

"This is perfect," Cammie continued. "Kill him with kindness on your blog and report your progress for the next twelve days."

Julia wasn't keen on this. The less exposure to Cain Maddox she had, the better. "I don't know . . ."

"The countdown is sure to attract attention to your blog. All you need to do is to be kind to him. You're naturally friendly and funny. This guy won't know what hit him. And then you can document what happens on your blog. Mark my words, readers will love this."

"Did you even hear what I said?" Julia reminded her friend. "I can tell you right now kindness isn't going to affect him one way or the other."

"You won't know until you try."

Julia bit down on her lower lip as visions of winning that highly paid position swirled in her head. Maybe Cammie was right. Maybe this idea would be just what she needed to generate a following that would show off her communication and writing skills.

"I think people are responding to my blog about Christmas decorations."

"Julia, do you have any idea how many people blog about making homemade tree ornaments? You're no Martha Stewart. You need something fresh and fun. A subject that will pique interest, something different—and frankly, wreathmaking isn't it."

Surely there was a better way to tackle this challenge. Showing kindness to someone she disliked wouldn't be easy. In addition, she sincerely doubted it would make any difference. The man was annoying, disagreeable, and stubborn.

"You aren't saying anything," Cammie said, interrupting her thoughts. "Which, from experience, I know is a good sign. You're actually considering doing this, aren't you?"

Bouncing her index finger against her mouth, Julia said, "I suppose killing him with kindness is worth a try."

"It totally is. And you can title your blog 'Twelve Days of Christmas.'"

Truthfully, Julia wasn't convinced this would work.

Cammie had no reservations, though. "It could inspire an entire movement."

"I'll give it some thought."

"Good. Gotta scoot. Scottie's eating the cat's food again."

Julia smiled as she disconnected, picturing the toddler eagerly stuffing cat food into his mouth while his mother was sidetracked on the phone. Cammie was a great ideas person, and Julia appreciated her friend's insight.

Bottom line: Julia didn't know how much longer she could hold out working in menswear at Macy's. The holidays were the most challenging. Her hours were long and she was required to work in the wee hours of the morning on Black Friday, which meant she hadn't been able to fly home for Thanksgiving.

Spending time with her family over Christmas looked to be a bust, too. Her parents would have been happy to pay for her airfare, but at thirty-one, Julia didn't feel she should rely on them to pick up the expense. Besides, she had commitments.

As her church's pianist, she was needed to accompany the choir. The talented singing group had scheduled a few special appearances, the last of which was coming up this weekend. She was grateful her boss had agreed to let her schedule her hours around those obligations. In addition, Julia was a volunteer for the holiday program at the Boys and Girls Club.

The bus continued to plug along as her thoughts spun with ideas. Julia gazed out the window, admiring the lights and the window displays along the short route that would take her to the very heart of downtown Seattle. She really did love the holidays. It was a special time of year.

Maybe she could treat Cain Maddox's surly mood with extra doses of nice. It would be an interesting test of the power of kindness. As a bonus, she wouldn't need to stress about content for her blog. She would simply be reporting the results. Easy-peasy.

But being impulsive had gotten her into trouble before, and so Julia decided to mull it over before making a final decision.

—

By the time she returned to her apartment that evening, it was dark and miserable, with drizzling rain and heavy traffic. Her feet hurt and she was exhausted. These long holiday hours at the store were killers.

Killers. Hmm . . . her mind automatically went to her neighbor. Killing him with kindness. It was a shame that Cain Maddox was such a killjoy.

Not wanting to fuss with dinner, she heated a can of soup and ate it with her feet propped up in front of the television. She caught the last of the local news broadcast. The weatherman forecast more drizzle.

In the mood for something to lift her spirits, she turned off the television and reached for her phone. A little music was sure to do that. Besides, it would be good to familiarize herself with the songs for the performance coming up this weekend. Scrolling down her playlist, she chose a few classic Christmas carols, the ones the senior citizens seemed to enjoy the most at the choir's last performance at an assisted-living complex.

Julia sang along with the music as she washed the few dishes she'd dirtied and tidied her apartment. Music had always soothed her. She sang loudly through her personal favorites: "Silent Night." "O Little Town of Bethlehem." "It Came upon the Midnight Clear."

She was just about to belt out "Joy to the World" when someone pounded against her door. The knock was sharp and impatient. Determined.

Oh dear. Julia hoped her singing hadn't disturbed anyone.

She opened the door wearing an apologetic smile and

was confronted by her nemesis from across the hall. Cain Maddox. She should have known.

His eyes snapped with irritation.

"What can I do for you?" she asked, doing her best to remain pleasant.

He continued to glare at her, his scowl darkening his already shady eyes. It was a shame, too—he was an attractive man, or he could be if he wasn't constantly frowning. She noticed he had a high forehead above a shapely mouth. Her father claimed a high forehead was a sign of intelligence, which was ridiculous. The only reason he said that was because his forehead was high. The thought caused her to smile.

"Is anyone dying in here? Because that's what it sounds like."

Holding her temper was a challenge. "Are you referring to my singing?"

"Tone. It. Down."

Not please, not thank you, just a demand.

With one hand still on her apartment door, Julia met his stare. "It's music. Christmas music, to be precise."

"I know what it is," he said with a groan, and briefly slammed his eyes shut.

"Would I be wrong to suggest that a kind, gentle soul such as yourself objects to a few classic Christmas carols?" she asked, ever so sweetly. Her words flowed like warm honey.

He glared at her as if she'd spoken in a foreign language. "All I ask is that you cut the racket."

"Please," she supplied.

"Please what?"

"Please cut the noise," she said with the warmest of smiles, fake as it was.

"Whatever." Cain shook his head as if he found her both irritating and ridiculous. She searched for a witty retort but couldn't think of anything cutting enough to put him in his place.

Before she could respond, Cain returned to his own apartment and slammed the door.

"Well, well," Julia muttered under her breath as she closed her own door. Perhaps Cammie was right. This man desperately needed help, and she was just the woman to see to it.

She'd kill him with kindness if it was the last thing she ever did.

Inspired now, she took out her laptop and sat down on the sofa. Making herself comfortable, she stretched out her legs, crossing her ankles. Booting up her computer, she went to her blog and saw that only fifty people had logged in to read her latest post. So far her efforts weren't going to impress anyone. Most of those who read her blog were family and friends. The solitary comment had come from her mother.

Julia's fingers settled over the keyboard, and she typed away.

Julia's Blog

TWELVE DAYS OF CHRISTMAS

December 14

Meet Ebenezer

I'm wondering if anyone else has encountered a genuine curmudgeon this Christmas season? The reason I ask is because I believe Ebenezer Scrooge lives in my apartment building. To be fair, he hasn't shared his views on Christmas with me personally. One look and I can tell this guy doesn't possess a single ounce of holiday spirit. He just so happens to live directly across the hallway from me, so I've run into him on more than one occasion. To put it mildly, he's not a happy man.

Just this morning I discovered he was something else:

A thief.

I caught him pilfering my newspaper. Really, does it get much lower than that? Well, as a matter of fact, it does. This evening, not more than a few minutes ago, I was confronted by said neighbor demanding that I turn down the

Christmas "racket." I happened to be singing. He claimed it sounded like someone was dying.

When I complained about him to a friend—and, okay, I'll admit I was pretty ticked off at the time—it came to me that this coldhearted "neighbor" is a living, breathing Scrooge.

My friend, who is near and dear to my heart, suggested *I kill him with kindness.*

So, my friends, I hope you'll join me in this little experiment. I fully intend to kill my surly neighbor with the love, joy, and fun of Christmas. Naturally, I will keep his identity confidential, referring to him only as Ebenezer.

I'm not exactly sure where to start. If you have thoughts or suggestions, please share them below. I'll be updating this blog every day until Christmas. Hopefully, by then, this Grinch's heart will have grown a few sizes.

My expectations are low.

I'm not convinced kindness can change a person.

We'll find out together.

I welcome your comments and ideas . . .

Chapter Two

First thing the next morning, Julia checked her blog and smiled when she saw that she already had fifty views and ten shares. To her delight, there were three comments.

MagpieMurphy: Good luck. This should be interesting.

That first comment was from a college friend who had faithfully been reading her blog and supporting her efforts.

The second comment was from a new reader.

JingleBellGirl: The best gift you can give during the holidays is HOLIDAY CHEER. I'm excited to read your blog. Good luck.

The last comment was from an unfamiliar name as well. As far as she could see, she had at least two new readers.

DerekDude120: Don't waste your time . . . once an Ebenezer, always an Ebenezer.

Julia knew exactly what she wanted to do for her first kindness experiment. She'd come up with the idea before falling asleep. She showered and dressed and collected both Cain's and her newspapers.

She rode the elevator back up to her floor and then knocked on Cain's door. She heard a loud bark from the other side, followed by his muffled voice a few moments later. "Who is it?"

"Your neighbor," she returned, gushing with charm. "Padden. Julia Padden." She did a poor imitation of James Bond.

Silence, followed by "What do you want?"

"I come bearing gifts."

"I'm busy."

"No problem. I'll lean it against your door."

"Lean *what* against my door?"

"You'll see. Don't you like to be surprised?" she called out.

The door flew open and he stood in front of her, his face covered in shaving cream, with a razor in his hand. His leg blocked Schroeder from jetting into the hallway. The Irish setter's tail wagged. His master might not be friendly, but Schroeder was. Cain's gaze narrowed. "I don't like surprises."

"Here's your newspaper."

He grumbled and took it out of her hand and tossed it onto the table next to his door.

"You're welcome," she said pointedly at his lack of appreciation.

Turning away, she was fairly certain she heard him grumble, and knowing she was getting his goat, she added, "Have a good morning."

"Whatever."

She grinned. "You say that a lot, don't you?"

"Would you mind? I'd like to finish shaving."

"Of course." Julia did her best to keep her voice friendly and good-natured. This was working so well, she could barely stand it. Cammie was right. Kindness was going to torment him, and the truth was, Julie really wanted to annoy him the same way he annoyed her.

With a game plan in mind, she returned to her apartment and waited until she heard his door open as he left for work. Making it seem like pure coincidence, she stepped out of her apartment at the same time and met him at the elevator.

"We meet again," she said in a cheerful voice that would rival Mary Poppins's.

His gaze narrowed at her before he looked away.

She smiled when she noticed he had his morning newspaper tucked under his arm. It was then that she noticed a piece of tissue stuck to his chin. He'd apparently cut himself while shaving. Her eyes widened. "I hope my interruption wasn't responsible for you nicking your face."

"No." Cain impatiently hit the button for the lobby for

the second time, as if that would cause the elevator to descend faster.

"Those little cuts can be annoying."

"So can pesky neighbors," he muttered.

Julia smiled. Oh, this was good. "I don't mean to be pesky. I was just collecting my newspaper and thought I'd get yours at the same time. I'm happy to do that for you. I'll set it outside your door and give a gentle knock so you know it's there."

"Don't."

"Don't knock?"

"Don't get my newspaper."

"Why not? I'm getting my own. It isn't any trouble."

"Just. Don't."

"Okay, if that's what you want."

As soon as they reached the lobby and the elevator doors slid open, Cain made his escape. Looking at him rushing away, one would think he was running for his life.

"Have a good day," she called after him and waved. As soon as he was out of sight, she nearly doubled over with laughter. He couldn't get away from her fast enough. This was turning out better than she'd hoped.

Feeling like she'd made progress, she decided to treat herself to a latte at the corner Starbucks. Luck was with her, and she noticed that Cain was three people ahead of her in line.

Unable to resist, she called out loud enough for him and the entire crowd to hear. "Cain, I didn't know you came here for coffee. I can pick one up for you some morning, if you'd like."

He glanced over his shoulder and she could have sworn she heard him groan.

Phil, Julia's favorite barista, looked up and waved. "Morning, Julia."

She raised her hand and wiggled her fingers back at him. "Morning. That's my neighbor. I'd like to buy his coffee."

If she hadn't gotten Cain's full attention before, she did now. He whirled around so fast he nearly knocked the man behind him off balance. His gaze shot straight to her. "I'll buy my own coffee."

"It's my way of apologizing for tormenting you with my Christmas music last night."

Phil looked from one to the other, then handed Cain his coffee.

"I'll pay for my own coffee," Cain reiterated, and slapped the money down on the counter.

"Okay, if you insist. I'm just really sorry for disturbing your peaceful evening with my cheerful Christmas music." A lie if there ever was one.

He walked past her and was out the door a moment later.

Interested in what Phil could tell her, Julia leaned forward as soon as she reached the counter. "Does that guy come in here often?"

"Most every morning. He always orders the same thing. Never says much."

"That's what I thought." Not exactly a surprise or the kind of info she was looking for. "Do you know anything else about him?"

"Not really," Phil said. "He never talks to me or anyone else that I've seen."

Julia had assumed as much. She placed her order and then paid for Cain's coffee for the following morning in the form of a gift card.

"Tell him it's from me," she said, almost giddy with excitement.

Phil willingly joined in with her scheme. "He seemed pretty adamant he didn't want you buying his coffee."

"I know. He's not exactly the friendly type."

"I noticed," Phil said as he wrote her order out on her cup. "I'll make sure I'm at the register in the morning. I'll keep the gift card here and use it then."

"Perfect. Thanks, Phil."

"His reaction should be interesting." The barista's eyes widened.

That's exactly what Julia was hoping. "I just wish I could be here to see it."

Once she'd collected her drink, Julia had to hurry to the bus stop in order to catch the bus. As it was, she was the last one to board.

The woman was driving Cain nuts. And he wasn't falling for that sweeter-than-honey smile of hers, either. No one was naturally that perky in the morning. She had to be doing this for the sole purpose of getting a reaction out of him.

She might be cute—to be honest, more than cute—but

he wasn't willing to play whatever game she'd conjured up to torture him.

His best option was to ignore her, which he fully intended to do. Walking briskly now, he headed down the street to the Harvard Insurance Company. He'd specifically chosen his apartment building because it was within easy walking distance of his job. This offered him the opportunity to return to the apartment for lunch and take Schroeder out. He felt bad that he had to leave the Irish setter cooped up for the majority of the day. Thankfully, the dog was getting on in years and slept most of the time, anyway.

When his grandfather had gone into the assisted-living complex, he was only allowed to bring dogs weighing twenty pounds and under. Schroeder was a brute at sixty-five pounds. Bernie refused to leave Schroeder until Cain offered to give him a home himself.

Cain's thoughts drifted to his grandfather. He loved the old man who'd raised him. Now that Bernie was close to eighty, his health had started to decline. To his credit, though, Gramps had adjusted well to his small apartment. Unlike Cain, his grandfather made friends easily.

Even as a boy, Cain had been reserved, quiet, and intense. His job as an actuary suited him. Numbers made sense to him, unlike people. He rarely allowed anyone to get close, and for good reason. It seemed every time he did, he regretted it. All he had to do was remember how Dani had betrayed him. But he wasn't going there.

"Morning, Mr. Maddox," the front-desk receptionist

greeted him, the same way she did every day. He noticed she'd put up a small Christmas tree on the counter.

He tipped his head, said "Morning," and continued past.

He couldn't remember her name if his life depended on it. That was just the way he liked it. His life was organized and structured, and there was no way he was going to let his vivacious, irritating neighbor disrupt that. He paused as he stepped into his office and closed the door. If he chose to ignore his neighbor, then why was he wasting time thinking about her now? It was a good question, and one he was reluctant to answer.

Once at Macy's, Julia had a good day and suspected it was the distraction of her experiment with Cain. The shoppers didn't seem to be as frenzied or impatient as usual. She made sure to wish everyone a Merry Christmas and had her best sales to date. After work, she headed off to the Boys and Girls Club to help her friend Jeremy with the youngsters as they prepared their holiday program. The kids were great and Julia enjoyed her time with them. She had just enough time to get from the Boys and Girls Club to church for choir practice.

The choral group enjoyed spreading a bit of Christmas cheer and joy to those who were often ignored or forgotten. The previous week they'd sung at a soup kitchen after volunteering to serve meals. This week they would perform at Manor House, an assisted-living complex in the city. By the time Julia finished up at the church and made it back to her apartment, it was eight-thirty and she was pooped.

Stopping by the mailbox in the lobby, she was collecting her assortment of bills when she noticed someone had joined her. It was Cain. He must have come from the gym, because he wore Nike workout gear and had a white towel dangling around his neck. She'd never noticed how buff he was. That was a pleasant surprise, although it shouldn't have been.

Ignoring her, Cain checked his mailbox, and seeing that he had no mail, he closed it. He paused then, and glanced at her as if he expected her to comment.

Julia would have if she wasn't exhausted. She'd spent eight hours on her feet, and then an additional two hours playing piano. The energy to be witty and cheerful wasn't in her.

They silently rode the elevator together. He stood as far to one side as he could, and she did the same on the other side. Julia could feel his gaze on her, almost as if he expected her to say something and was suspicious when she didn't. When they reached the third floor, they each went to their respective doors.

She started inside her apartment but paused when she felt his scrutiny. Looking over her shoulder, she noticed him staring at her, frowning.

It almost seemed as if he was concerned about her lack of chatter. She managed a smile. "Have a good evening, Cain," she said.

To her surprise he returned, "You okay? You don't look so good."

She managed a smile. "It's been a long day."

He nodded curtly and disappeared inside his apartment. Silly how a short, innocuous comment excited her. She wasn't even entirely sure whether this was progress or not. It felt promising, though.

Sitting on her sofa, laptop in hand, she opened her blog and saw she had more than a hundred hits, along with twelve comments. Wow. She read the comments and took notes. Some of the ideas were great.

SassySusan: I love your thinking and totally agree that killing Ebenezer with kindness would be perfect. Rub his nose in cheerfulness and goodwill.

Julia's Blog

TWELVE DAYS OF CHRISTMAS

December 15

The Mailbox Encounter

Operation Kill Him with Kindness continues . . . Tormenting him with my cheerful chatter: check. I'm fairly certain he gritted his teeth when he saw me this morning.

Phase Two: I brought him his newspaper and purchased his coffee for tomorrow with a Starbucks gift card. It'll be interesting to see how he reacts to that.

A curious development this evening. We met in the lobby when I was collecting my mail, purely by coincidence. From previous experience, I had the feeling he would do just about anything to avoid me. It goes without saying that I am not his favorite person, though I'm not sure this guy likes anyone. Scrooge, remember? I'm certain my attention has him utterly confused, not to mention how I've pretended to ignore his rude responses, including every cold shoulder. I'm sure he doesn't know what to make of me.

So I gave him a little cold shoulder myself this evening in an effort to keep him on edge. And because I was too tired for much else. Then, and this is what I found interesting, as I unlocked my door I felt his gaze on me, almost as if he was waiting for me to speak. When I looked back, I saw him studying me as if he was disappointed that I hadn't gushed with my usual charm.

I wonder if I'm getting to him. Could it really be possible? So soon? It's been only two days!

I'll close for now. I appreciate the comments. And to HattieHomemaker, who wrote, "Sweeten him up with peanut butter cookies. Works with my husband every time." I think you're onto something . . .

Chapter Three

Cain hated to admit it, but his irritating neighbor was beginning to get to him. He stood with Schroeder in the dark while waiting for the dog to do his business, his head full of Julia. Determined as he was to put all thoughts of her out of his mind, he found it nearly impossible. He hadn't been able to stop since their chance encounter the night before.

When he saw her collecting her mail, he felt fairly certain she was only then getting home from work. She'd had one long day. Nothing said how exhausted she was more than the fact that she hadn't burst into jovial babble the instant she saw him. By all that was right, he should count his blessings. At every other meeting, calculated or by chance, she'd brightened up like a yellow canary and started chirping like the cage door had unexpectedly sprung open.

Cain hadn't meant to comment and regretted that he had. He cherished the peace and quiet of the elevator. Then he saw how slowly she walked to her apartment door. The deciding factor came when she'd looked over her shoulder at him with a weary expression. Cain hadn't been able to help himself.

It was her eyes, round and hopeful, as if all she needed was a kind word from him to restore her. Fool that he was, Cain had given in and then instantly regretted it. Their short conversation was sure to lead to more conversations, and he wasn't interested in being neighborly or anything else. Julia needed to stay on her side of the hall, and he would gladly do the same.

As a result of his slip in judgment, Cain had spent a restless night convinced he'd given Little Ms. Sunshine all the encouragement she needed to force-feed her sweetness into his life. Well, that wasn't going to happen.

Schroeder let out one sharp bark and Cain realized his dog was eager to get back to the warmth of the apartment.

"Sorry, buddy," Cain murmured. "Be sure you're done, because I won't be back at lunchtime. It's Bernie's birthday, and I need to buy him a gift. I was thinking about a sweater. You got any better ideas?"

Schroeder stared up at him blankly.

"That's what I thought. A sweater will have to do."

Schroeder led the way back to the apartment. If he hurried through his morning routine, he just might escape riding the elevator with her.

—

Julia suspected Cain was probably looking to avoid her at the elevator. She was equally determined to make sure she manipulated it so they left at the same time.

She was ready and waiting when she heard movement across the hallway. That was her cue. She lingered until he reached the elevator before coming to stand beside him.

When he saw her, Cain's shoulders sagged in defeat. Her responding smile was genuine. "Ah, we meet again," she said, grinning gleefully back at him. "It seems we leave about the same time every morning."

"I noticed, and I don't think it's coincidence."

He had a small scab forming from his shaving cut the morning before.

"I didn't get your newspaper this morning, as you requested."

He kept his gaze up, focused on the floor numbers.

"Looks like we're in for another day of drizzling rain. Does the rain bother you?"

"Not particularly."

"Me neither."

"Are you always this chipper in the morning?" he asked.

"Always."

"Would it be possible for you to tone it down a little?"

She swallowed a smile. "I can try."

"It would be appreciated."

The elevator stopped on the second floor and an elderly gentleman Julia didn't recognize got on.

"Morning," she greeted.

"Morning," the older man said and inclined his head toward her.

Julia looked over at Cain. "So you go to Starbucks nearly every morning."

His gaze narrowed. "How'd you know that?"

"Phil told me."

"Who's Phil?"

"The barista." The fact that he didn't know Phil said he hadn't paid even minimal attention to the waitstaff.

"Daily Starbucks doesn't fit into my budget," Julia continued, "but I manage to treat myself once or twice a week. Have you ever tried their peppermint mocha? It's one of the seasonal specialties. It's the best."

"You're chattering again."

"Sorry. I'll try harder to get a grip on that," she said, and pantomimed zipping her lips closed.

The elevator door opened, and once more Cain rushed out like a bat escaping a cave, determined to get away from her.

"Have a wonderful day," Julia called after him, offering him a small wave, although he couldn't see her. Once more, as soon as he was out of sight, she struggled to smother a laugh.

She wasn't sure she was supposed to enjoy this experiment this much; certainly it was more fun than she'd thought it would be. Because she was a few minutes early, Julia stopped to chat with Eddie, who manned the front desk, complimenting him on the Christmas tree and other holiday paraphernalia that decorated the lobby, before heading to the bus stop.

Phil must have seen her waiting outside, because he came out of Starbucks a few minutes later, wearing a big grin. Julia was excited to see him, wondering how Cain had reacted to her gesture for a cup of coffee.

"So," she said, even before he reached her. "What happened?"

He handed Julia the gift card. "He refused to accept it."

"That figures." It didn't surprise her, but she was disappointed.

Phil gave her an odd look, as if he wasn't sure he should even ask the question. "Are you interested in this guy? You know, romantically?"

A horrified look came over her. "You're joking, right?"

"Well, it certainly seems that way. If you are, I'd advise you to save your breath. He's one cold fish."

"I'm looking to spread a little Christmas cheer is all," she explained, unwilling to talk about what she was doing or her blog.

"I don't think this neighbor of yours is into Christmas."

That would be Julia's guess as well. She didn't expect he would be, which was sad. She didn't understand how anyone could not appreciate Christmas. As the lyrics of one of her favorite Christmas songs said, it was the most wonderful time of the year.

"I better get back inside," Phil said. "I'm on break."

"Thanks again. I appreciate the help."

"Yeah, no problem; I'm sorry it didn't work out."

"Me, too." She hadn't expected Cain to accept, but part of her had hoped that he would. It would've shown a small crack in the armor he wore like a second skin. Despite everything, she wanted to think he wasn't immune to kindness.

Phil started to leave but then turned back. "He asked about you."

"Cain did?" She saw the bus approaching and groaned. "What did he want to know?"

"Sorry, I've got to get back inside and it looks like your bus is here. We'll connect later."

"Later," she echoed, disappointed. It would be telling to learn what Cain had asked Phil about her.

Julia's phone rang just after she clocked in to work at the department store. Seeing it was Cammie, she decided to answer. She had an extra five minutes before she needed to be on the floor.

"Hey," Julia greeted her. "What's up?"

"What's up is you!" Cammie said excitedly.

"What do you mean?"

"You have two hundred views on your most recent post."

"I do?" Julia did a mental happy dance. "Really?" It'd been up only a few hours. This was unprecedented.

"I'm telling you, this blog idea is catching on," Cammie continued. "It will win you that contest for sure. You've as good as got this job, my friend."

"And just think, it was all your idea."

"You're killing him, Julia."

She loved hearing it. She mentioned the gift card Cain

had refused from Starbucks earlier and that he'd asked about her.

"When will you see Phil next?" Cammie asked right away.

"I don't know . . . I guess I could stop in tomorrow morning."

"Do. You need to find out what Cain was asking."

Her friend paused, and it was almost as if Julia could hear Cammie's mind spinning.

"I bet he's hot for you."

"Not happening," Julia countered swiftly. "First off, he sees me as a nuisance. Fact is, I'm pretty sure he cringes any time he sets eyes on me."

"Pretty sure he's interested. Dig what you can out of Phil."

Julia wasn't convinced that was such a great idea. As it was, the barista had already suggested that she acted as if she was romantically interested in Cain. That was definitely a path she didn't intend to take.

One thing she did find fascinating, though, was the fact that this experiment had been going on for only a couple days, and already it appeared to be having an effect on Cain.

As soon as she ended the conversation with Cammie, Julia headed out to the floor. Holiday shoppers waited outside the doors, and as soon as Macy's opened, the crowds rushed in for the latest bargains.

Although she worked almost exclusively in menswear, Julia found that seventy-five percent of her customers were women. Many were seeking presents for the men in their lives. One of the few things Julia enjoyed about her job was helping others find the perfect gift.

The morning sped by and Julia stopped for lunch. While she sat in the break room, she read over the comments from her blog. Several of her readers offered her encouragement and advice. Some swore they had neighbors exactly like Cain and were implementing their own experiments.

Seeing the interest her blog had generated in only two days encouraged Julia. She owed Cammie for this idea.

JingleBellGirl: Keep up the chatter!

#Chatter4Christmas: Maybe try kicking it up a notch with an elf outfit tomorrow.

Julia smothered a laugh. She could just imagine Cain's face if she did.

SassySusan was back as well, with a comment.

I love that you bought him coffee—bet he drinks only straight drip, and of course no sugar. He doesn't like Christmas carols? Who doesn't like Christmas carols? He needs sweetening up. You might try fudge.

When she returned from lunch after one, she noticed that the displays were a mess. Seeing that the other sales staff were busy with customers, Julia took the opportunity to straighten the stack of sweaters that were currently discounted for the holidays.

"Excuse me, do you work here?"

The voice was all too familiar. It couldn't be. No way. Slowly she turned, and she couldn't hold back a huge smile. How did she get so lucky?

Cain was Christmas shopping? This she had to see.

"Yes, I do," she said, and beamed him a smile.

His eyes widened when he saw it was her. An entire slew of emotions crossed his face, and for a half-second Julia thought he might make an excuse to leave.

"How can I help you?" she asked.

He continued to stare at her. "Is this a joke?"

"What do you mean?" she asked with a look of innocence, her hands folded in front of her.

He shook his head as if he didn't have an answer, or more likely would rather not say.

"I work for Macy's, and I'd be happy to help you, Cain."

He nodded as if he were a man accepting his fate and facing a hangman. "I need a man's sweater."

"Do you have a price in mind?"

"Not really. I want to make sure it's comfortable and warm. That's my only requirement."

"Okay, what about color? Do you have a preference?"

"Blue."

"Size?"

"Medium."

She'd asked because she'd noticed how broad Cain's shoulders were. The man was stacked, and in a good way. She'd paid attention earlier, but even more so now. What a shame that he pushed people and relationships away. With a personality transplant he would have the potential to be more than eye candy. To use a bit of a cliché, a smile would certainly increase his face value. "Is it for you or someone else?"

"Why do you want to know?" he asked, as if she'd overstepped her bounds as a salesperson.

It would be easy to take offense, but she didn't. "Because," she returned calmly, "if you were purchasing the sweater for yourself I'd suggest going up a size. You have broad shoulders. I noticed you work out. It shows."

He didn't let on if he appreciated the compliment, not that she suspected he would.

"Flattery, Julia?"

She hadn't been sure he even knew her name. That he would say it was a nice surprise. "It's a compliment."

He didn't let his feelings be known one way or the other. Instead, he answered her question. "The sweater isn't for me."

She motioned toward the table where she'd been straightening out the inventory. "These are good-quality sweaters and they're on sale. We have higher-end choices as well, if you're looking for something in cashmere."

"These will do," he said, and then added, as if it pained him, "I appreciate your help."

Dismissing her, Cain sorted through the sweaters, which left Julia to wait on another customer. She kept half an eye on him as he searched the pile until he found what he wanted. It wasn't until she'd finished with the other customer that she remembered that Cain had thanked her. It was almost as if the words pained him to get out. Any sort of appreciation from him was an improvement. He'd never thanked her before. In fact, when she'd delivered his newspaper the day before, she'd been obliged to prompt him.

This was a small victory, and one she savored.

It just so happened that she was at the register when Cain approached a few minutes later. Julia had trouble holding back a smile at the look that came over him when he realized it was her.

"I see you found what you wanted," she said. "This is a good choice."

"Thanks." He reached into his back pocket for his wallet and paid with cash.

"Would you like a gift receipt?" she asked, as a matter of course.

"No."

"A gift box?"

"No." He glanced at his wrist as if to suggest he had limited time.

She handed him his purchase. "Merry Christmas, Cain."

He held her gaze and then muttered, "Bah humbug."

Julia couldn't help it; she laughed. "You don't like Christmas?"

"Truth is, I don't have any feelings good or bad over Christmas. It's something to be endured."

Endured? Christmas? She held his look for an uncomfortably long moment. "I think that's one of the saddest things anyone has ever said to me."

He shrugged, as though it was of little consequence.

"Can I do anything to make Christmas better for you?" she offered.

He shook his head. "No thanks."

"That's twice now that you've thanked me."

"You're keeping tabs?"

She returned with the same gesture he'd given her: a shrug. "You aren't free and easy with your appreciation."

"I'll get right on that."

His voice was emotionless, but Julia saw the teasing light in his eyes. She planted her hand over her heart. "Cain Maddox, you have a sense of humor. Who would've guessed?"

He did smile then. This was progress, real progress, whether Cain was willing to admit it or not.

Cain returned from visiting Bernie and was happy his grandfather liked his birthday gift. The minute he stepped off the elevator he smelled something baking. One of the last memories he had of his grandmother was of her baking him chocolate-chip cookies. Every time he smelled that aroma he felt a sense of loss. Even now, as an adult, he experienced a pang at the memory.

His life had fallen apart after the death of his grandmother. His mother had abandoned the family when he was little more than a toddler. His father hadn't been able to cope with him, and within a few short weeks he sent Cain to live with his grandparents. He remembered crying for his mother and his grandmother holding and rocking him. Whenever he was sad or had experienced a bad day, she baked him chocolate-chip cookies.

The first day of junior high he'd gotten into a fight and was sent to the principal's office. His grandfather had been disappointed and lectured him. In an effort to smooth over matters, his grandmother had baked him his favorite cookies, and since her death he'd never touched them again. It was a tribute to the only woman who'd ever loved him.

Sure enough, Cain wasn't home more than thirty minutes when Julia showed up at his door.

Schroeder barked, just in case Cain hadn't heard her distinctive knock. He'd heard it, all right, and would like nothing better than to ignore it.

"Cain," she called out. "I know you're home."

One would think she'd get the message, but apparently that was too much to hope.

"What is it now?" he asked, doing his best to hide his irritation as he flung open the door.

Julia blinked at his lack of manners. What did she expect? By now she should know he didn't welcome company. Instantly, he regretted his childish behavior and relaxed his shoulders. She looked adorable in a Santa hat and a cute Christmassy apron.

His appreciative glance was all she needed to proudly hold out a plate of chocolate-chip cookies. They were wrapped in green cellophane and tied up in a pretty white bow. When he didn't immediately accept her offering, she said, "I baked these for you."

"Thanks, but no thanks."

Immediately, the smile drained out of her eyes. "You don't like cookies?"

"No."

"Oh." She didn't back down. "In that case, maybe you'd like to take them into the office with you," she suggested.

Her big blue eyes pleaded with him, only this time he wasn't giving in. "Why don't you take them in to work yourself?" he countered.

For a long moment she remained standing just on the other side of his doorway, as if she had trouble believing he would turn down her cookies. "I suppose I could do that," she admitted reluctantly.

"Good." Now that it was settled, he started to close the door.

"These are some of my best cookies," she tossed out, cocking her head to one side in order to see him as he closed the door.

He ignored her. He'd say one thing about Julia, she was persistent. In all the years he'd avoided chocolate-chip cookies, this was the first time he'd ever been tempted. And that didn't settle well with him. In fact, it completely unnerved him.

Julia's Blog

TWELVE DAYS OF CHRISTMAS

December 16

Meet the Man Who Turns Down Cookies

What man in his right mind turns down warm-from-the-oven chocolate-chip cookies?

Ebenezer does.

You read that right. I baked him cookies, dressed up in a cute little elf apron, which he clearly didn't appreciate, and my Santa hat. I couldn't have looked more festive if I'd tried.

Maybe I'm trying too hard.

Every time I start to make progress, my hopes build, only to be slammed to the ground like an ocean wave over-taking a sand castle.

As you can tell, I'm frustrated.

But I'm getting ahead of myself. I currently work for a large department store, and guess who came in shopping this afternoon? You guessed it, Ebenezer. Needless to say, he didn't look the least bit happy when he saw I was his salesclerk. But after I offered to help, he actually thanked me.

Oh, and one other important development: This morning, as I waited at the bus stop, I learned Ebenezer asked the barista about me. I repeat, Ebenezer asked about *me*!

The thing is, and I hesitate to admit this, I've actually started to care about him. Not in a romantic way, don't get me wrong, but as a human being. I mean, when I started this blog he irritated me to no end. I had no kind thoughts toward him. I actually looked forward to being a pest. Guess that doesn't reflect very well on me, does it? The reason I mention this is because it feels like I'm right back where I started, which is pretty discouraging. This man is cold, and I'm beginning to doubt that kindness can even touch him.

Chapter Four

Julia posted her blog and within five minutes she had dozens of hits and twenty comments. It seemed everyone had something to say. Several were helpful and some were downright funny.

> BelieverinLove: Don't be discouraged. The fact that he's fighting so hard shows you're having an effect on him.

> Ain'tGonnaTakeIt: Sneak rat poison into his coffee. Oh wait, he doesn't want that, either. Find a way.

> .

> SingleMom: I met someone like him. In fact, I married him. Run, sister, run, and don't look back.

Several comments boiled down to the simple message of: *Don't give up now.*

Reading the comments helped, so by the time Julia left to join the choir members Saturday morning, her annoyance with Cain had more or less dissipated. To her surprise, he was leaving his apartment at the same time she was.

He seemed equally taken aback to see her.

"You work on Saturdays?" she asked as they walked toward the elevator.

"No. You?"

"Not today." It seemed to take the elevator an extra-long time to reach the third floor. When it did arrive, he held open the door for her to precede him. So he could be a gentleman when so inclined!

"It's going to be a great day."

He arched his brows as if to question her. "I doubt that. Rain is forecast, the streets are clogged with traffic, people are pushing and shoving on the sidewalks, crazed with Christmas madness. If that's a good day for you, then you're a better person than I am."

"Thank you, Mr. Glad Tidings," she teased. "As you might have guessed, I love the holiday season." She waited, and when he didn't comment she added, "You forgot your line."

"My line?" He arched his brows in question as they reached the lobby and entered the foyer.

"Aren't you supposed to say 'Bah humbug'?"

For just a moment, fleeting as it was, she thought she saw him smile. If so, he quickly disguised it behind his usual emotionless expression. He shook his head as they left the lobby, but then he waited and held the glass door open for her.

"Thank you." That was twice now that he'd held a door for her, something he'd never done to this point. She supposed that was progress. Her readers would say these little signs should encourage her. And they did.

"You're welcome," Cain said.

They parted ways on the sidewalk. Cain went in one direction and she in the other. She made a brief stop in Starbucks, and to her disappointment discovered Phil wasn't working. She'd catch him later and hope he'd be able to remember his conversation with Cain. She needed to know what Cain was curious to find out about her.

Julia was one of the first to arrive at Manor House, the assisted-living complex on Beacon Hill. She wanted to be sure everything was set up and ready for the choral group and that the piano was in place. She'd visited earlier with the choral director and told the staff what they would need.

Sure enough, several rows of chairs were already arranged in a large area off the dining room. Many of the elderly patrons had to be escorted from their rooms. A number of them used walkers. Julia stood in the entry and greeted each resident as he or she progressed into the room, wishing them a merry Christmas.

Nothing could have shocked her more than when she saw Cain accompanying an elderly man. When he caught sight of her, his eyes narrowed with what looked like suspicion and doubt. After he got the older man settled into a chair in the second row, he walked over to where she stood.

"Could I talk to you a minute?"

"Sure."

"Not here," he said gruffly.

"Then where?"

He led the way down the hall and around the corner, out of sight of the residents and staff. "Did you follow me?"

Her eyes felt like they were about to bug out of her head. "Follow you? You mean here? Of course not. Why in the name of heaven would I do anything like that?"

"Then what are you doing here?"

Julia stiffened and did her utmost to remain calm and serene. "I have my reasons," she assured him. His arrogance was beyond measure.

"Are you stalking me?"

"You think I'm stalking you?" The idea was so ludicrous she burst out laughing. If the twitch in his jaw was anything to go by, Cain wasn't amused. "I find it all too convenient that you seem to turn up everywhere I do. First it's at Starbucks, then the lobby when I'm collecting my mail. And what's the deal with you just happening to be at the elevator every morning?

"I can't even shop without running into you. I don't know how you planned all this, but I want it to stop and I want it to stop now."

Julia closed her eyes before her temper blew, because if it did, he'd regret his accusations. When she'd composed herself enough to respond, she held up her index finger. "One, I was collecting my mail first. You intruded on me. Two." She held up a second finger. "You can rest assured I will take pains to avoid catching the elevator the same time as you from this point forward. I would rather miss my bus than ride with you ever again. And three." A third finger snapped up. "I'm clever, but not clever enough to arrange to be working at the exact place and time you decide to shop. And four." She breathlessly had four fingers up now. "I have every right to be in Starbucks. If you don't like it, then I suggest you get your coffee elsewhere."

Dragging in a calming breath, she added, "Now, if you'll excuse me, there's a reason I'm here and it has nothing to do with you." She started to walk away and then whirled back around to confront him nose to nose. "For the record, you're the most arrogant, unpleasant man I've ever known."

The experiment was over. She couldn't do it any longer. Stepping into the restroom, Julia locked the door and leaned against it. She took a few minutes to compose herself, holding her hands up to her face. Her cheeks were hot with barely restrained anger. It took several moments for her breathing to return to normal.

Knowing she'd be required to play for the singing group, Julia wetted a paper towel and pressed it to her face. When she felt like she could smile again, she came out of the restroom. The choral group had arrived and Julia slid onto the piano bench.

Mrs. Bounds, the choir director, stood before the audience and introduced herself.

"We are pleased to be here this morning to share a few of our choir's Christmas selections for your enjoyment. Julia Padden will accompany us on the piano."

Julia didn't dare look into the audience. For all she knew

Cain had left, which was what she hoped he'd done. The man was insufferable. Until fifteen minutes ago, she'd thought she'd made progress. It really was one step forward and ten steps back when it came to this jerk.

Mrs. Bounds faced the choral group, raised her arms, and then looked to Julia, whose fingers were poised over the piano keys. At Mrs. Bounds's signal, she started playing.

As always seemed to happen, she soon got immersed in the music and the tension evaporated from between her shoulder blades. Unable to resist, she looked to where she'd first seen Cain. He sat next to the same man she'd seen him with earlier. Their eyes locked, and for one intense moment the room faded away and it was just the two of them. The blank, emotionless expression that was his trademark had been replaced with a look of regret. Before she could read anything more, her attention was drawn back to the choir and Mrs. Bounds. Regretful or not, Julia was finished with him, with the experiment, with everything— even if it meant she would lose the chance at the Harvestware job. Her stomach was in knots. She desperately wanted the job, but not at the expense of her sanity.

When the performance was over, Julia stepped outside and called Cammie, who happened to be grocery shopping. It took her best friend all of two seconds to figure out she was upset.

"Julia, what's wrong?"

She blurted out the entire story and finished with "I'm giving up the blog."

"You can't," Cammie cried. "Have you looked at the

numbers on the post you put up yesterday? You've got over a thousand hits, with two hundred shares. Do you have any idea how big that is?"

"I just can't do it any longer," Julia insisted.

"You can," Cammie encouraged. "Think about it. Don't overreact. Yes, Cain is difficult and you have every right to be upset, but there's a reason he's the way he is. It's your job to find out what makes him tick."

"He's arrogant and—"

"Wasn't he all that before you started the blog?"

Her friend had a point, and as much as Julia wanted to argue with her, she couldn't. "Yes, I guess . . ."

"Then nothing has really changed, has it?"

Julia straightened. As much as she hated to admit it, Cammie was right.

"A thousand hits," her bestie repeated. That was way beyond the interest Julia had been able to generate before.

"People are loving your blog and this project. When you get a chance, read the comments posted in the last couple hours."

"I will, for sure." Julia tapped her foot while she considered this news.

"You say Cain accused you of following him?"

"Yes, the man is delusional." His accusation continued to enflame her.

"You could have claimed that he followed you, you know? Cain was there for a reason."

As always, Cammie had said exactly what Julia needed to hear. Cain hadn't shown up at the Manor House out of the blue because he was in the mood for a bit of Christmas cheer. She suspected he had a friend or a relative at the complex or was there out of some obligation.

"Thanks, Cammie. I'll check in with you later."

"Do that, and keep your cool."

"I will."

With a plan in place, she returned to the building and stepped up to the receptionist's desk.

"Do you have a resident here with the surname of Maddox?" she asked, doing her best to give the impression of goodwill toward all men.

The woman behind the counter smiled. "Yes, that would be Bernie. Nicest man you'd ever want to meet—charming and sweet."

Charming and sweet? Clearly he was no relation to Cain. She would have liked to seek out Bernie right then, but she feared Cain might still be in the building. She'd return at a later date and introduce herself and find out what she could about Cain, if indeed they were related. The more she knew about him, the better prepared she'd be to show him kindness, even if she had to do it with gritted teeth.

Before she was finished, Cain Maddox would rue the day he'd met her.

Julia's Blog

TWELVE DAYS OF CHRISTMAS

December 17

A Smile

My friends, I have a small confession to make. I nearly abandoned the project after my last encounter with Ebenezer. I've never met a more frustrating man in my life. He actually accused me of stalking him because I happened to be in the same place as him! Truthfully, it was sort of spooky. But stalking him?

Pullleeeease.

This experiment has gone from a mission to a battle, and at the moment the opposition (Ebenezer) is winning. A woman can take only so much. It just so happened that I had an excellent reason for being where I was. One he discovered soon enough. I know he regretted his accusation, but did he apologize? Did he admit he was in the wrong? Not Ebenezer. When I next looked for him he'd disappeared, and truthfully, that was probably for the best, because I wasn't exactly in a forgiving mood.

Then this afternoon, through no fault of my own, I inadvertently met Ebenezer in the lobby of our apartment building. I waited for him to accuse me of having prearranged that as well. Thankfully, he didn't. Instead, he seemed to be in a much better mood.

I, however, wasn't. I glared at him, daring him to say a single word.

You won't be able to guess what he did.

He smiled.

Yes, smiled as if nothing had happened . . . as if I should forget what he'd said and pretend all was right with the world. I, however, am unwilling to ignore his error in judgment.

And then. Then he added insult to my already injured pride, and he said he might find me attractive if I wasn't so cheerful in the mornings.

As if I would even want him to find me attractive!

Can you believe this guy? That did it.

I'm not quitting.

If anything, I'm going to be all the more merry and bright. I'll blind him with how upbeat and sunny I'm going to be.

What I didn't expect was that killing him with kindness would be the death of me. But I can do this, thanks to you and the encouragement you've given me.

Wish me luck.

Chapter Five

When Julia asked for encouragement, it came in the form of more than two hundred comments. This blog had grown at a shocking pace. By the following afternoon, her latest entry had more than three thousand views and five hundred shares in addition to pages and pages of comments.

Wow.

Even though it was the weekend, Julia checked the hallway before leaving the apartment for fear she might inadvertently happen upon Cain on his way out. It wasn't likely, seeing that it was Sunday, but she wasn't taking a chance. She'd taken Saturday off and therefore was working Sunday instead, which bummed her out. It was the holiday season, and the store and other sales representatives depended on one another to carry their own weight.

One day, God willing, she'd be able to work a nine-to-five job doing social media. Julia had to believe that or she'd be really depressed.

While waiting at the bus stop, Julia watched as her favorite barista shot out the door of Starbucks.

Phil was excited as he rushed up to greet her. "Julia, you'll never guess what!"

"What?" she said, watching as the Metro bus approached the stop.

"That guy. Cain, I think his name is. He was in earlier this morning and he bought you a drink. A peppermint mocha; said it was your favorite." Phil held up the drink for her to see.

"Cain . . . bought me . . . this?" She was so shocked she could barely get the words out. "You're kidding?"

"He said to give it to you the next time you stopped in, but I saw you waiting here and whipped it up. I thought you'd want to know."

"You said he asked about me the other morning," she said. "What did he want to know?"

The bus arrived and people started to board.

"He asked if you were always a cheerful pest in the mornings or if it was an act put on for his benefit. I told him you were always kind and friendly."

"Thanks, Phil."

"I didn't really answer his question and he noticed, so I don't know if that was any help or not. He might have thought I liked you because you're thoughtful enough to leave a tip. In retrospect, I should have told him you're upbeat and personable, because you are."

The bus driver leaned toward the open door. "You getting on or not?"

"I'll let you know if he asks anything more," Phil said. "I've got to get back inside."

"Yeah, later." Flustered, Julie took the Grande-sized cup Phil held out to her and boarded the bus. She found a seat and held on to the drink with both hands. Cain had bought her this drink, the very one she'd mentioned a few days earlier as being her holiday favorite. The way she figured, this was about as close to an apology as she was going to get.

This was big, as in GIGANTIC!

Clenching her fist, she nearly thrust her arm up and let out a shout of victory. The thick wall Cain had built around himself had cracked. Sure, he'd held the door open for her and given her a smile that looked like it pained him, sort of like he was trying to turn the top of a rusted-shut jar lid.

This peppermint mocha, however, was solid proof. Kindness was working, and she'd only begun to scratch the surface. She could hardly wait to tell Cammie. And update her blog! Her readers were going to eat it up.

Following her shift at the department store, instead of returning to her apartment to put her feet up and write Christmas cards, Julia made an impromptu visit to Manor House, the assisted-living complex where the choir had performed the day before.

The complex was beautifully decorated for the holidays.

Because of all the extra holiday hours she'd worked at Macy's, plus her volunteer efforts, she hadn't put up her own Christmas tree. Her plan had been to do it that very day, if time allowed.

The woman at the front desk looked up and smiled as Julia approached. "I'd like to see Bernie Maddox," she said.

"Are you a relative?"

"No. I was here on Saturday with the church group."

"Oh yes, that was lovely. The residents talked about it for a long time afterward. Everyone enjoyed the music." She glanced down at the resident sheet. "Bernie's in room 316, but I don't think you'll find him there."

"Oh, is he out for the day?"

"No, he isn't listed as having left the building. Bernie tends to spend a lot of time on the fifth floor, in the game room. My guess is that's where he'll be."

"Thanks," Julia said appreciatively. Then, fearing she might run into Cain, which in her opinion would be nothing less than disastrous, she asked, "He doesn't happen to have company, does he?"

The woman, whose name tag identified her as Sharon, shook her head. "Not that I know of."

"Okay, thanks."

"Bernie's one of the kindest residents we have, a real gentleman."

That would be a startling contrast to Cain Maddox. They had to be related, seeing that they shared the same surname.

Julia took the elevator to the fifth floor and wandered

down the wide hallway until she found the game room. Sure enough, Bernie Maddox sat at a large table, holding on to a piece of a jigsaw puzzle. After a careful examination, he set it back down and reached for another, studying it with a frowning intensity.

"Are you Bernie Maddox?" she asked, although she knew he was. He was the man she recognized with Cain from the day before.

Bernie glanced up. "That's me." His eyes narrowed briefly. "Do I know you? You look vaguely familiar."

"I was here yesterday with the church group. I played the piano."

"Oh yes, now I remember. What can I do for you?"

Julia pulled out a chair and sat down beside him. "I live in the same apartment building as Cain Maddox. Are the two of you related?"

"Cain's my grandson. Is he in any kind of trouble?"

Interesting that Bernie would ask that particular question. She was half tempted to explain that Cain was trouble, but that wouldn't have been fair. "No, no, at least not that I know of. Does he get in trouble often?"

"If he does, he doesn't tell me about it. You know Cain?"

Unsure how best to answer, she said, "Sort of. His apartment is across the hall from mine, so we see each other fairly often. Let me put it like this: Cain isn't exactly the neighborly sort."

"Sounds like my grandson. That boy has a bad attitude, especially when it comes to women. Been that way for a good five years." He paused and studied Julia, his eyes twinkling. "You got the hots for Cain?"

Julia's head snapped back in shock. "Ah . . . not really." The question flustered and caught her off guard. She could feel color invading her cheeks. "Cain's an . . . interesting person." She was unsure how best to describe him, which left her stumbling over her words.

"Giving you the cold shoulder, is he?"

"Something like that." Julia made a quick decision. She would tell Bernie about her experiment. "We had something of a run-in recently. Cain took my newspaper and, well, it made me so mad I complained to a friend. Cammie's got a big, generous heart, and she suggested the best way to deal with Cain was to kill him with kindness."

Her words hung in the air for an awkward moment before Bernie slapped his knee and laughed boisterously. "You're killing Cain with kindness? Tell me, how's that working for you?"

"At the moment not so well, although I got a bit of encouragement this morning."

"Oh?" Bernie was all ears.

"Cain bought me a mocha from Starbucks." She explained the circumstances of how he'd arranged it for her.

The old man's eyes widened. "He went to all that trouble? Seems to me you're getting him good, girl."

"It isn't like that." Julia felt she had to explain. "I believe this is about as close as Cain's going to get to apologizing to me for the way he acted yesterday."

Bernie's face folded with concern. "What did he do yesterday?"

Julia told him how Cain had accused her of following him and had basically warned her off.

"Why'd he think that?"

She explained that as well, which meant at this point she'd done the majority of the talking. That wasn't so bad, except she'd come to learn what she could about Cain. Instead of being upset, Bernie chuckled. "In other words, you've been in his face for the last few days. I can just imagine his reaction to that. You've made escaping you nearly impossible for my boy. Wonderful. I love it."

"He doesn't make it easy. I baked him cookies, which he refused."

Bernie shook his head. "Bet they were chocolate chip."

"They were."

"Thought as much. He won't eat them, but I'll gladly take them. Been a month of Sundays since I tasted home-baked cookies."

A good portion of the batch had gone into the break room at Macy's, but she'd held back a dozen or more. Bernie was a dear, just the way the receptionist claimed. Julia decided then and there to make sure the remainder went to Bernie.

"I delivered his newspaper to his apartment, too . . . until he demanded that I stop."

"Not even a thank-you?"

"No."

Bernie grinned. "Seeing as he left you that fancy coffee drink, my guess is he's struggling with what he feels."

"I make sure we leave for work around the same time each morning." It wasn't like Cain could avoid her. "But I won't any longer." She'd been determined earlier, but not after this latest episode.

Bernie frowned. "Why not?"

"Well, because . . . he thinks I'm stalking him."

"You listen to me, Julia. Don't you change a single thing. If he doesn't want to take the elevator with you, then he can always use the stairs."

Julia liked the sound of that.

"Cain doesn't like me much," she confessed. "That's fine. I didn't really expect he would." Although she wasn't willing to admit it, she'd started to have feelings for Cain. Not necessarily romantic ones; she found that she wanted to know more about what made him tick.

"Think you're wrong about that," Bernie said with a thoughtful look. "He's attracted to you, but knowing my grandson, he's fighting it tooth and nail."

"Doubt it. He said I'd be far more attractive if I wasn't so cheerful in the mornings."

Bernie laughed so hard, Julia was afraid he was about to fall out of his chair. "That boy hasn't got a romantic bone in his body. He probably thought he was giving you a compliment."

Julia wanted to clear up any misconception. "I'm not interested in Cain romantically."

Her comment sobered Bernie in quick order. "Why not? He needs a pretty girl like you in his life."

Rather than explain that Cain Maddox was the last person on earth that she'd date, she said, "He isn't open to a relationship—not with me, at any rate." And from what she'd seen of him, not with anyone.

"He's interested. I know my grandson. You might not

realize, it but buying you that frou-frou coffee was a major concession on his part."

Julia thought it best to change the subject. "Can you tell me why Cain's so . . . standoffish?" She searched for the right word. *Standoffish* sounded better than *cold* or *mean-spirited*, both of which she'd once considered him to be.

Bernie's amusement faded quickly. "The boy hasn't had an easy life. His mother abandoned him when Cain was around four. Our son knew nothing about raising a child on his own so he brought Cain to me and my wife. Carl, that was our son, was brokenhearted after his wife left him. He never did recover emotionally nor did he bond with his son the way he should have. He felt guilty about that and after a while he stopped coming around."

"Oh." Basically, both Cain's parents had abandoned him.

Bernie continued, "Cain needed his father. I tried to fill in as best I could, but it wasn't the same."

Julia was beginning to feel terrible for judging him.

"Then our son died in a car accident. Cain was about twelve at the time. He took his father's death hard."

"Did he ever connect with his mother?"

Bernie shook his head sadly. "Fortunately, my grandson was close to my wife, but then she died about three years after Carl."

"Oh dear." Julia sank lower in the chair.

"Her illness came at a crucial time in Cain's life. He was going into high school, and until that point had always gotten good grades. I'm afraid I wasn't much help, grieving as I was."

Julia placed her hand on Bernie's arm. "I'm so sorry."

"It's years ago now. One adjusts, although you never fully recover from the loss of a loved one. I sort of figured out a way to walk around that black hole in my life. I did the best I could, but it wasn't near enough. Thankfully, he wasn't the kind of teen to get into trouble or anything like that. He sank into himself, grew quiet and withdrawn. It's like he's afraid to let anyone too close for fear they'll abandon him."

Julia was almost afraid to ask the following question. "Has Cain had any meaningful relationships?"

"Romantic ones, you mean?"

She nodded.

Bernie rubbed the side of his face as he mulled over the question. "He doesn't share a lot with me. After his grandmother's death, Cain seemed to turn off his emotions, sort of the same way his father did when Gayle left him. I know there was this one woman a few years back. They worked together. Cain became a mentor to her, and then I suspect they became more. How much more I can't say, but I do know Cain was serious about her for the simple reason he mentioned her a few times. It encouraged me that he was willing to open himself up. Then there was nothing and the light went out of his eyes."

"What happened?"

Bernie shook his head. "I was never completely sure, but reading between the lines, I got the impression that this woman cozied up to him in order to gain his favor for a promotion. I assumed once she got what she wanted she dumped him."

Julia briefly closed her eyes. That explained a lot.

"I've asked him about his social life, but he refuses to answer or quickly changes the subject."

Every ugly thought Julia had entertained about Cain vanished. Learning about his family and the woman who'd used him for her own personal gain changed her perspective.

"Now you can see why I think this kindness experiment you mentioned is exactly what my grandson needs."

"I feel terrible."

"Why?" Bernie asked.

Julia was sure guilt was written all over her face. "I haven't exactly been thinking kind thoughts about Cain."

"No worries. Those will come in time."

The comment struck her as odd. "They will? What makes you say that?"

"You'll see." Right away he changed the subject. "By chance, do you happen to know how to play cribbage?"

"I do. My grandfather taught me."

Bernie's face lit up like a Christmas Eve candlelight service. "You got time to humor an old man?"

"Sure. You think you can beat me?"

"I can try."

Julia ended up spending an hour with Bernie, the cribbage board on the table between them. Bernie was happy to tell her story after story about Cain until she felt she knew far more about him than she'd ever imagined she would.

"Cain ever mention his dog?"

"You mean Schroeder?"

"No, Bogie."

"No, I can't say that he has." But then they weren't exactly on the most friendly terms.

"Raised Bogie from a pup. Loved that dog like he was human. The two of them did everything together. Bogie lived until he was eleven, which is old for a large dog. Devastated Cain when we had to put him down. I wanted him to get another dog, raise him, too, but Cain refused. Said he'd had his dog."

"But he has Schroeder now."

"Schroeder was my dog. Couldn't have him here at Manor House, so Cain agreed to take him. I know he sees to his needs, but I worry that Schroeder isn't getting the TLC he used to." He looked to her as if she could tell him what he wanted to know.

"I can't say, but I do know Cain walks Schroeder every day."

Bernie's expression sobered. "Cain doesn't show a lot of emotion. He keeps the way he feels locked up inside. I'm hoping this kindness project of yours will make a difference. It's what he needs and a lot more."

They played several games of cribbage. It'd grown dark by the time Julia prepared to leave. She collected her coat and purse and thanked the older man. "Bernie, I had a wonderful afternoon. I can't thank you enough."

"The pleasure was mine. Can't remember the last time I've enjoyed a visitor more. I hope you'll come again."

"I will, and I'll bring you those cookies next time I stop by."

"Wouldn't turn them down like my foolish grandson."

Leaning forward, Julia kissed his weathered cheek. "It might not be a good idea to mention our visit to Cain."

"Not a good idea at all," Bernie agreed. "Keep me updated on your progress. A twelve-day experiment, you say?"

"Twelve days. This is day five." For a number of reasons she didn't mention the blog, mostly because it didn't seem relevant. She wasn't sure he would even know what a blog was.

"I'll stop by again soon."

"Good. I'll look forward to that more than you know. Furthermore, I demand a rematch," he said, putting away the cribbage board. "Your grandfather did a good job teaching you; you're one fine opponent."

Julia considered that high praise.

Despite the hour, Julia stopped off at a Christmas tree lot on her way back to the apartment and purchased a large wreath and a small tree. It was awkward getting both home on her own, and when she got to the elevator, she saw a sign that read: TEMPORARILY OUT OF ORDER.

"Just great," she muttered under her breath, her shoulders sagging with defeat. It'd been a long day and she was dead on her feet.

"What is?"

Cain stood behind her, a take-out bag in his hand.

Julia shot him a look. "The elevator is out of order."

A huge grin came over his face. "Looks like you're up a creek with a Christmas tree."

She paused, unable to look away. Cain was an attractive man when he smiled. And, while she hated to admit it, he was good-looking even when he didn't, which in her humble opinion was grossly unfair. "This isn't funny."

"On the contrary. I look forward to watching you haul that tree up two steep flights of stairs to the third floor." He walked over to the door leading to the stairs and held it open. "You coming?"

Julia wasn't about to give him the satisfaction. "Go on ahead of me. You wouldn't want your dinner to get cold, would you?"

"And miss seeing you struggle with that tree? Not on your life."

"I'm happy you think this is amusing."

"Come on," he urged, tilting his head toward the stairwell. "I'm not a doorstop, you know."

Julia dug her fist into her hipbone. "In case you hadn't noticed, I could use some help here."

Cain cocked his eyebrows. "Do you want me to contact the building manager for you?"

The man was infuriating. Ignoring him as best as she could, Julia carried the bushy fir tree into the stairwell. The Christmas tree might not be big—it was less than four feet tall—but it was heavy. Determined to ignore him, she marched up the first few steps and was halfway to the second floor before she had to pause and rest the base of the tree on the concrete step. Leaning against the railing, she glared at Cain. He was seriously going to let her do this on her own. If nothing else, it would make great blog material. No one would doubt it was a true Ebenezer moment.

"I suppose I should thank you for the mocha," she said while gathering her breath.

"Collected it already, did you?"

"Phil brought it out to the bus stop for me this morning. Peppermint mocha's my favorite; you remembered."

Crossing his arms, he seemed perfectly content to wait for her.

"I should have refused it," she said, stiffening.

"Why would you do that?"

"You did."

He wagged his finger like a pendulum. "Different situation."

"Whatever. What about the cookies? You refused those, too."

"I'm watching my weight."

He didn't have a spare ounce of fat on him. That was an excuse if ever she heard one. In other circumstances she would have called him on it. At least they were talking, and while it might not be the most fun conversation, it was an improvement over the last couple days.

She hauled the tree up the rest of the flight and paused on the landing. "I hope you realize that comment about me stalking you was low."

He shrugged. "It was."

"Are you going to apologize?" She challenged him with a hard look.

Cain met her gaze and for a half-second it looked as if he was in danger of smiling. "How about I help you haul that tree up to the third floor instead?"

Julia was no fool. "Deal."

He took the tree out of her hand and effortlessly climbed the remaining stairs. Julia followed behind with the wreath and was breathless by the time they reached their floor. Cain stood outside her door while she dug in her purse for her keys.

"Were you serious about not getting in the elevator with me again?" he asked as she inserted the key and opened her apartment.

"I've had a change of heart, not that we need to worry about meeting at the elevator now that it's out of order."

"Good point."

"If by chance it's working tomorrow morning and I happen to leave for work the same time as you, then I would suggest you either take the stairs or wait."

He cocked his head to one side. "You wouldn't want me to be late for work, would you?"

She gave a nonchalant shrug. "Your choice."

"I'll take the elevator with you," Cain said as he carried the tree into her apartment. "Where do you want this?"

"By the window." She had to analyze what he'd just said. "Are you saying you don't mind my sunny disposition and cheerful chatter?"

"That isn't what I said."

"Then what did you mean?"

Ignoring her question, he leaned the tree against the window. "You have a tree stand?"

"I do. You didn't answer my question."

He frowned. "About catching the elevator? It's just what I said. I don't want to be late for work, and I wouldn't want you to miss your bus."

"You could leave earlier, you know."

"You could, too. No biggie. Do whatever makes you comfortable."

Cain would rather submit to torture than hint that he enjoyed her company.

"Are you going to get that tree stand or not?" he prompted.

Leaving him, Julia went into her bedroom and stretched up to the top shelf of her closet and brought down the box of Christmas essentials. Including the tree stand.

"Here," he instructed once she returned. "Hold on to the tree and I'll get it set up for you."

Julia grabbed hold of the center of the tree while he knelt down on the floor and fitted the trunk into the stand.

"I appreciate the help," she told him, and she did. It amazed her that the day before she'd been ready—eager, even—to throttle Cain Maddox. The difference in his attitude toward her from one day to the next was shocking.

"Cain?"

"What?" he muttered.

"Why are you helping me?"

He leaned back on his haunches and looked up at her, frowning. "Would you rather I didn't?"

"No. I'm surprised is all."

He leaned forward, flattening his hands on his thighs. "If you must know, I decided you don't have any untoward intentions toward me. I don't know what this Merry Sunshine act you've got going is all about, but I've sort of gotten used to it."

Julia did her best to hide a smile.

"You go overboard, but I can live with that."

"Big of you," she muttered.

He chuckled. "I decided you were right. You couldn't possibly have known I needed a birthday gift for my grandfather and planted yourself in the Macy's men's department."

"Nor did I follow you to Manor House."

"Right."

Returning to setting up the tree, he fiddled with the screws in the stand as he spoke. "You have to admit you have been making a pest of yourself."

"You really didn't say that!" It was agonizingly slow progress with this guy.

"I'm not being critical, but it seems you're hard up for a man."

Her mouth shot open. "Hard up for a man," she repeated, as the outrage built until she was afraid she was going to explode.

"Don't get me wrong. I'm flattered."

Julia let go of the tree and it fell over sideways, hitting her small kitchen table before bouncing to the floor.

"Hey," Cain barked. "Why'd you do that? I've got three of the four screws in."

"Out," she shouted, and pointed toward the door.

A look of bafflement came over him. "What's your problem?"

"First off, I am not hard up for a man, and if I was, I can assure you that you'd be the last man in Seattle who would interest me."

His eyes crinkled with a smile. Something he didn't do nearly often enough. "Evidence says otherwise."

"Thank you, Sherlock." In thinking about it, Cain must assume she was blatantly flirting with him. It would be hard to convince him otherwise. Seeing how she'd repeatedly made efforts to get his attention, it sort of made sense. She hadn't considered that when she'd taken on this experiment.

"Get over yourself, Julia. Do you want me to get this tree in the stand or not? Your choice."

Julia weighed her options. She could remain mad and then struggle to get it up on her own or swallow her pride and let him do it. "Okay, fine, finish."

Cain straightened the tree and Julia clasped the middle of it while he adjusted the last screw. She remained tight-lipped, unwilling to hand him additional ammunition to use against her.

Cain broke the silence with a question. "How long have you been playing the piano?"

"I thought you considered music noisy racket." He'd made a big scene about it only a few days ago.

"I had a bad headache that night."

"Oh."

"I suppose you're looking for an apology for that, as well as everything else."

"Not particularly."

"Good, because I wasn't going to give you one." He finished and leaned on his haunches again. "Is it straight?"

Julia stepped back and examined the tree before she nodded. "It is. Thank you."

"I'd say it was my pleasure, but it was more a pain in the butt."

"Then why did you do it?" He really was the most exasperating person.

"Well, for one, you needed help, and for two, I'm a bit taken aback to find I don't dislike you nearly as much as I thought."

Julia laughed and pressed her hand over her heart. "Who knew?"

"Knew what?" he asked, looking up at her with a quizzical expression.

"That you could be such a silver-tongued devil."

Cain laughed. He bounced back to his feet and grabbed his take-out bag. "See you in the morning."

Not until her apartment door closed did Julia realize he was basically telling her he'd meet her at the elevator.

Julia's Blog

TWELVE DAYS OF CHRISTMAS

December 18

He's Not My Type

Wow, do you know how to have a girl's back! I read all of your comments and suggestions and want to thank everyone who contacted me. And never fear, I'm filled with more determination to continue than ever.

And guess what? The biggest encouragement I got came from Ebenezer himself. Yes, you read that right. The thick wall around this unpleasant man has showed its first major crack. He bought me a latte, which I'm sure was his way of letting me know he regretted his accusations from Saturday.

Talk about being surprised. It's almost as if he's reading this blog himself (which I can assure you he isn't), and he gave me all the incentive I need to continue.

Furthermore, he's talking to me now. I mean talking as in a regular conversation other than terse one-word answers.

I learned something else from him, something he told me himself. He asked if I would be at the elevator in the morning. Simple question, right? After the fiasco on Saturday, I'd been determined to rearrange my schedule so we wouldn't meet. I went so far as to tell him so.

While he didn't come right out and admit it, he looks for me now. He actually looks for me. And while he might still complain about my morning cheerfulness, I believe he secretly enjoys it.

Oh, and I met his grandfather and got some insider information. As I suspected, Ebenezer had a woman do him wrong. That has apparently soured him on relationships. No surprise there, right?

When he was helping me set up my Christmas tree he implied I'm romantically interested in him and actually said that I was hard up for a man. I guess he couldn't go more than a few minutes without irritating me. I did my best to hold my tongue—far be it from me to be accused of flirting with him. He's really not my type.

No way.

Not interested.

Will report back tomorrow.

Chapter Six

Julia sort of hated to admit it, but she was looking forward to seeing Cain on Monday morning. She listened at
her front door for what seemed like forever, but he didn't
show. Her goal was to make it look like their meeting up at
the same time every morning was pure accident. It wasn't,
of course, and she'd pulled this little trick more than once.

As time ran out, with no option left, she had to leave or
miss the bus. Cain was a no-show. Either he'd left earlier
than normal or he was running late. The temptation to tap
on his door was strong, but she resisted.

Giving him the wrong impression about her intentions
made Julia extra-cautious. Letting him think she might be
interested in him romantically wasn't part of the experiment. Still, he'd made a point about the two of them con-
necting that morning. She couldn't help but wonder what

the deal was. Knowing him, it was probably a ruse to keep her guessing and on her toes. That would be just like Cain.

The closer it got to Christmas, the crazier her workday became. Shoppers crowded the store, searching out the perfect gift at the best price. Being this busy made the time pass quickly for Julia.

During her lunch break, she barely had time to grab a few bites as she read the comments on her blog. The number of hits had doubled.

Doubled.

SassySusan: See? Knew it was working. So glad you stuck with your plan. Met his grandfather, did you? Devious little devil you turned out to be.

JingleBellGirl: Who says he's not your type? He bought you a latte. What more do you want?

And the comments went on for pages. People were loving this project and giving her all kinds of encouragement. What her readers liked and mentioned most was the latte Cain had gotten her. Like Julia, her readers saw the fact that he'd gotten Julia her favorite drink as a seismic shift in Cain. This one action was proof that killing him with kindness was working even better than they had hoped. To Julia's way of thinking, it had taken far longer for that crack to show itself than she would have liked. Nevertheless, she'd take it.

Although she hadn't given the Christmas-tree incident more than a casual mention, several of the readers picked up on that as well. As far as Julia could tell, Cain didn't oppose Christmas, he just wasn't into it. In retrospect, that made sense. For many years now it'd been just him and his grandfather. It wasn't like he had an extended list of people he needed to shop for or a big family. Knowing what she did, she had an idea.

As soon as she was finished with her shift, Julia took the bus to Manor House to see Cain's grandfather. She'd packed the last of the homemade chocolate-chip cookies to bring him that morning, but that was just an excuse to seek him out a second time in as many days.

Sharon, the woman who was at the reception desk at Manor House, smiled when she saw Julia.

"You're starting to become a regular, aren't you?"

"Guess I am," Julia called out as she rushed past. "Bernie's in room 316, isn't he?"

"Probably not."

She skidded to a stop. "Oh, is he up in the game room again?"

"Could be. Check there first."

"Will do. Thanks." With a wave and a jaunty step, Julia was off to the fifth floor. Sure enough, she found Bernie sitting at the table, working on the same jigsaw puzzle he had been the day before. Two other men were off in the corner, playing cribbage, she noticed.

Bernie glanced up, and when he saw her, his face immediately broke into a smile. "You're back."

"Promised you home-baked cookies, didn't I?"

"You brought them?" His eyes widened with delight.

"I sure did." She set her bag down on the tabletop and brought out the plastic container with the cookies.

"You sweetheart. If my grandson was foolish enough to refuse these, then I'll gladly accept them." Right away he peeled off the cover and snatched a cookie. After a single bite, he closed his eyes as if tasting ambrosia. "Better than I imagined. Almost as good as the ones my wife baked, God rest her soul."

"Thanks." She pulled out a chair and sat down. "I didn't run into Cain this morning." Missing him had weighed on her mind most of the day. It seemed Cain wasn't the only one who'd grown accustomed to their morning ritual.

"He's sick," Bernie mentioned casually as he reached for a second cookie.

"Sick?" That was a shock. "I saw him last night and he seemed well enough then."

Cookie in his hand, Bernie looked up. "What time was that?"

"I don't remember. Around seven, I think. Why?"

"Wasn't feeling great then, either. He usually stops by Sunday afternoon, but he didn't want to give me whatever it was that upset his stomach. Surprised he didn't mention it when he saw you."

"He helped me haul my Christmas tree up the stairs." Then, because she felt she needed to explain, she added, "The elevator was out of order."

"Talked to him this morning and he sounded sicker than a dog. From what he said, he spent most of the day in bed. Guess it's the flu."

"Oh dear." Julia immediately felt terrible. What little she knew of Cain told her he wasn't a man who took easily to being ill.

"You okay?" Bernie asked.

"Fine." She brought her head back to the present. "I had an idea. Don't know if you and Cain have plans for Christmas Day?"

"Nothing more than dinner right here at Manor House. What makes you ask?"

"How about you come to my apartment? I'll be alone, and it would be a good excuse for me to cook."

"You a good cook?"

"Good enough. Living alone, I don't get much practice," she explained, "but I have my mother's and grandmother's Christmas recipes." She welcomed the excuse to host dinner for Bernie and Cain.

"You going to serve more of these cookies?"

"I can make that happen."

"Turkey and the fixings?"

"Whatever you want," she assured Bernie.

"Count me in." He chuckled.

"What's so funny?"

"You being kind to Cain and me reaping the benefits."

Julia smiled. "Cain might refuse once he finds out it's me, you know."

"Let him. If the boy wants to turn down a home-cooked Christmas dinner he can, but I'm no fool."

Julia glanced at her wrist for the time. She was scheduled to be at the Boys and Girls Club to help with their practice for the holiday program. "Gotta scoot," she said.

"Thanks again," Bernie said, as she collected her purse and bag. "You feel free to stop by anytime."

"Will do."

"You don't even need to bring cookies. Your pretty smile is enough to brighten this old man's day."

Julia had taken an instant liking to Bernie. Just like Sharon claimed, he was a real sweetheart. Leaning forward, she kissed his cheek. "I'll visit again soon."

Bernie pressed his hand to his cheek. "Not shaving for a week," he told her, grinning ear to ear.

The practice with the kids at the Boys and Girls Club went well. Julia accompanied them on the piano as they rehearsed their songs for the program, which was scheduled for the night of December 23. She'd come to know a number of the children involved and admired the staff. Julia was grateful for the opportunity to volunteer. She liked the work they did with the neighborhood kids and enjoyed making this one small contribution.

"Really appreciate this," Jeremy Craig said when the practice was over.

They'd dated briefly, earlier in the year. Nothing serious. Julia liked him well enough and he seemed to feel the same, but there wasn't a spark between them, and it was foolish to pretend there was.

"Glad to do it, you know that."

Jeremy hugged her and walked her to the exit. "You walking again?"

"It's only a few blocks."

"Not sure I'm comfortable with that."

"Jeremy, it's perfectly safe. This is a good neighborhood. I've never even had a hint of a problem. The streets are well lit and there are businesses along the way. Nothing's going to happen."

"Okay, okay."

"Besides, I've taken karate classes." She had, but that had been a few years back and she'd had to stop after three lessons. The way she figured, when the time came and she needed to defend herself, her training would kick in. She hoped that wouldn't be necessary, but if it was she would be prepared.

She hoped.

On the walk home Julia passed the deli where she often grabbed something quick for dinner. The owners knew her by her first name. Although she wasn't especially hungry, she went inside.

Right away Levi acknowledged her with a raised arm. It was past the dinner hour and business had slowed to a few lingering patrons eyeing the variety of selections behind the glass case.

"What do you have that's good?" Julia asked, looking through the case herself. Levi made the best salads imaginable, but she had a weakness for his soups, which he cooked daily himself.

"What I got that's good?" he repeated in a heavy New York accent. "Everything is good."

"True enough."

He leaned against the case, his weight on his hands as he waited for her to make her selection.

"What's the soup today?"

"Chicken noodle."

Julia's head came up. Chicken soup was exactly what Cain needed. "Give me a quart of that."

"One quart of soup coming up."

Julia scanned the salads, but nothing appealed to her.

"Anything else I can get you?"

"I'm good." Julia remained full from lunch. She'd boil herself a couple eggs once she got home.

She paid for the soup, and her steps were filled with purpose as she headed back home. Getting the soup to Cain while it was still hot was a priority. Once inside the building, she dropped off her coat and purse at her apartment and went directly across the hall to Cain's. Schroeder probably needed to be walked, too. She'd volunteer to do that as well.

She knocked on his front door.

No response.

"Cain, it's me," she called, pressing her ear to the door. Sure enough, she heard him moving on the other side.

"That's supposed to entice me to open my door?" he grumbled.

She couldn't let him know she knew he was sick. "Come on, open up," she said when he ignored her summons.

"Go away," he told her.

"Not going to happen. I want to know why you didn't meet me at the elevator this morning."

"Why do you care? I'm avoiding you."

"No, you're not. If you remember, we specifically talked about it. I want to know what's up."

The lock turned and he cracked open the door. "I'm sick."

She exhaled a deep sigh as if this was news to her. "I thought that must be the case."

"Why'd you think that?" The door remained only slightly ajar, just enough for him to talk to her without shouting.

"Like I said, I just figured something had to be wrong when you weren't at the elevator this morning. Now, are we going to talk through a crack in the door or are you going to let me in?"

"No. Go away."

"What about Schroeder? Does he need to go out?"

"The building manager took him out."

"Come on, Cain, I thought we were past this. Let me in."

He grumbled something under his breath that she didn't quite hear. From what she could make out, it was a good thing she didn't pick up on all of it.

Reluctantly, Cain opened the door all the way and she entered his apartment.

When she did, she stopped short. "Whoa, you look horrible." And he did. He was deathly pale and his eyes were rheumy. If that wasn't enough, his hair was a mess; he wore sweats as if he was fighting a chill. His feet were covered in white sports socks.

"Okay, you've verified—I'm sick. Now leave."

She held up the container of soup. "I brought you dinner."

"Don't want it. Now go."

Julia set her hand on her hip. "Why are you so anxious to be rid of me? Well, other than you've never been all that happy to see me."

He frowned as if to say that wasn't entirely true. Not any longer. She doubted he'd ever admit it, but the look on his face said it for him.

"In case you haven't figured it out, I have the flu. Do you want it, too?"

"No worries. I had my flu shot." Not wanting to argue with him, she wove her way around him and stepped into the kitchen, which was in bad shape. Dishes filled the sink and food items were spread across the counter, including used tea bags and a multitude of cups. Ignoring the mess, Julia brought down a bowl.

"Julia, I'm serious."

"So am I," she said over her shoulder. She set the bowl and the container of soup on the counter and pried off the lid. Right away the room was filled with the aroma of chicken and noodles. "Have you had anything to eat today?" she asked as she filled the bowl with the hot soup.

"No."

"That's what I thought. Sit." She motioned toward the counter, where he appeared to take all his meals.

Again he grumbled, but he did as she asked. She stood on the other side of the counter and opened and closed the drawers until she found the silverware and then handed him a spoon.

Glaring at her, Cain took a tentative sip of the soup while Julia watched him. His look suggested that the faster he ate, the faster he could be rid of her.

"So?" she asked, with her hands braced against the edge of the counter.

"So what?"

"Hits the spot, right?"

He nodded. Guess that was a victory, although a small one.

"I need to lie down."

"You should." His sofa was a mess. He'd apparently spent the majority of the day there. Without asking, she went over to the couch and folded up the blanket and fluffed up the pillows.

"When did you turn into a regular Florence Nightingale?" he asked as he made his way to the sofa.

She checked her watch. "About ten minutes ago. I'll be right back." She left and returned a few minutes later with yellow rubber gloves, a plastic bucket, and cleaning disinfectant.

"What are you doing now?"

"Cleaning."

His frown was ferocious. "Don't."

She glared back at him.

"You're going to do it, anyway, aren't you?"

"Yes."

He closed his eyes and groaned. "If I had the strength I'd argue with you."

"You'd lose, so save your breath."

His apartment was the mirror opposite of her own, so she knew right where to go.

"Julia," he shouted, with a cutting edge to his voice. "You're upsetting me."

"I know. I'll be done with these dishes in a minute and then I'll take Schroeder out."

It seemed all the fight had gone out of him. "Okay." A couple moments later he shouted, "I thought you said you were nearly finished. What are you doing now?"

"Nothing."

He was up from the sofa, following her around. Cain closed his eyes as if battling within himself. "God save me from stubborn women."

"Pray harder," she told him cheerfully as she went about, remaking his bed and straightening his coverings.

For a moment it looked like he wasn't going to move. He blocked her path out of the bedroom.

"I hope you know that if I wasn't so weak I wouldn't put up with this."

"I know. You helped me and I'm simply returning the favor."

"When did I help you?"

How quickly one forgot. "With the tree, remember? You carried it up the stairs for me and helped me set it up."

He rolled his eyes as if to discount what he'd done.

"And I appreciated it. We had a nice conversation, too."

His frown was firmly in place. "I don't appreciate this."

"Didn't think you would." It went without saying if circumstances were any different he would never have put up with her pushy behavior. "You finish the soup?"

His answer was clipped and sharp. "Yes."

"Good. Bet you feel better, too."

"Taking the Fifth on that."

She grinned. "Figured you would."

"I don't need you fussing over me, and I definitely don't want you getting sick. Go away."

Julia's heart leapt at his words. "You don't want me to get sick? So nice that you care."

"Cut the bull, Julia. What I need is rest and sleep, and you're disturbing both."

"Give me a few minutes and then I'll leave you in peace. Deal? I've been sick before; I know what it feels like."

His shoulders sagged. "In that case, leave."

"Yes, sir. Right away, sir. Anything you say, sir."

He cracked a smile, although she could see he struggled not to let her know he was amused.

"You're a pain in the butt." Cain waited by the front door until she finished stacking the dishes in the dishwasher and turning it on. "What's taking you so long?" he demanded.

"Patience, my dear man, patience."

"In case you haven't figured it out, that's in short supply."

"Sort of guessed as much," she said as she moved out of the hallway. "I'll be back in thirty minutes with Schroeder."

"Just go."

She was actually enjoying this. "I'm only trying to help. You'd do the same for me."

"No, I wouldn't."

"Yes, you would. Now, where's Schroeder's leash?"

"Top drawer in the laundry room." His impatience was clearly evident. "Just go, would you? I need to lie down again. I'm feeling a bit dizzy."

"Do you need help?"

"What I need is to lie down, which I can't do with you irritating me."

She left Schroeder and placed her arm around his waist. "Let me help you back to the sofa."

It surprised her when he didn't make a fuss and allowed her to lead him across the room. He sank down onto the sofa, and Julia had to admit he looked dreadful. She found it hard to leave him, and she looked for ways to linger.

"I thought you were going to walk the dog?"

"I am." She didn't have an excuse to delay any longer.

As promised, she took Schroeder for a long walk. When she returned she found Cain had propped open the door and was asleep on the sofa. For a long time she simply stood and stared at him, fascinated by him and the shift in their relationship in the last few days. She'd softened toward him, and he'd had a change of heart toward her, too. It was subtle, and while they continued to bicker, it was often in jest.

He must have felt her scrutiny, because his eyes fluttered open. "Hey."

"Hey," she said softly, sympathetically. "I didn't mean to wake you."

He blinked a couple times and sat up. "I'm actually feeling better. Not sure if it's the soup or the scent of pine."

Julia smiled. "Maybe a little of both."

"Maybe."

"Can I get you anything?" Surprisingly, she found herself reluctant to leave. Just as surprising, he seemed equally hesitant for her to go.

"I don't need anything, but . . ." He paused.

"But?" she prodded.

"Would you like to watch TV with me?"

"Sure." All in the name of getting to know him better, she told herself.

"I'll let you decide what to watch as long as it isn't one of the animated Christmas specials."

"My, my, aren't you accommodating," she teased.

Cain grinned. "Don't know that I'm up to watching *Rudolph the Red-Nosed Reindeer* is all."

They spent an hour together and sat in companionable silence. In the best of times Cain wasn't much of a talker, and that was fine. Julia found she enjoyed herself with Schroeder huddled at their feet.

Cain thanked her when she left.

"See you in the morning," she said. "If you're feeling better, that is."

"I'm feeling worlds better already. Thanks for the company."

She should actually be the one thanking him, only he didn't know that or the reason why.

Julia's Blog

TWELVE DAYS OF CHRISTMAS

December 19

*Just Because I'm Nice Doesn't Mean
I'm Falling for You*

I'm halfway through this adventure and finally I feel like I'm making substantial headway. My day started off with a disappointment. Ebenezer was a no-show at the elevator, even after he said he'd be there.

You read that right. He stood me up.

I nearly missed my bus waiting for him. The whole way to work I stewed. It was just like him to pull a stunt like that—leading me to think he was softening to the pleasure of my company and then pulling this disappearing act. The pleasure of my company is a stretch, but you get my point.

Later I discovered Ebenezer was sick with the flu.

I hate to admit how excited I was to learn this, and not for the reasons one might assume. Yes, it explained why I didn't see him this morning, but it's more than that. What a perfect opportunity to show kindness, right? I couldn't have come up with a better plan if I tried.

He wasn't happy to see me, and that is no exaggeration. I brought him chicken noodle soup and he ate it, all the while complaining and demanding I get out of his apartment and leave him alone. I even cleaned for him, using disinfectant.

Naturally, he was gruff and impatient, which I anticipated. Really, it would have been foolish of me to expect anything less.

But here's the kicker. When I quietly returned to his apartment, Ebenezer was dead to the world on the sofa. (FYI, he snores.) He woke and asked if I'd like to stay and watch television with him. On his couch. Just the two of us, watching TV for an hour, maybe more . . .

Can't wait to see what Day Seven turns up . . .

Chapter Seven

Julia posted the blog. Within minutes of hitting the enter key, comments started appearing on her laptop screen. It was almost as if her readers had been waiting for her post. She watched in utter amazement as the number of hits mounted. It was hard to believe how enthralled people were with this kindness project.

Some of the comments humbled her. Julia's original intention hadn't been all that wonderful. She found Cain to be nothing less than an irritant. If not for Cammie, she would never have thought to do anything more than ignore him the same way he ignored her.

Then she read:

#Blessyou: I want to thank you. I started reading this blog on the third day, when a friend from work shared it with me. My mother-in-law and I have never gotten along. She has never liked me and didn't think I was good enough for her son. For the last five years we've barely tolerated each other. After reading your blog I decided I should try this kindness approach. I know she likes angel figurines, and I saw one on display at a flower shop and bought it for her. (Trust me when I tell you this woman has never been an angel to me!) After work I drove to her house and gave it to her. I could tell she wasn't sure what to make of my unexpected visit. I told her she was probably right that I wasn't good enough for Jack, but with her guidance maybe she could help me be the wife she envisioned for her son. To my astonishment, she threw her arms around me and started crying and apologizing. I wouldn't have believed peace between us was even possible. I have you to thank.

Mandy: You actually washed his dishes? Come on, girl, you're smarter than that. If he wants to live like a slob, let him. That is just plain wrong on so many levels I don't even know where to start.

Julia finished reading the comments and was overwhelmed herself. She closed her computer and sat staring into the distance. It was late, well past the time she should be in bed, but her mind wouldn't let loose of what was happening with her blog and between her and Cain.

After about fifteen minutes, she ran a hot bath and soaked in it while her mind whirled with the assortment of reactions, especially how much she'd enjoyed sitting with Cain and Schroeder and watching television together.

Chilled after getting out of the tub, she dressed in her fleece pajamas and headed for bed. She could feel a headache coming on and took two aspirin, determined to get a good night's sleep.

Julia woke at about three and immediately knew she was sick.

Desperately so.

She was barely able to toss aside the covers and rush into the bathroom in time to lose her dinner.

Oh no. This couldn't be happening; it just couldn't.

She had the flu.

Groaning, she stumbled back to bed and curled up in the fetal position. She'd had her flu shot. She should have been protected. Getting sick wasn't supposed to happen. To complicate matters, her week was crammed with commitments and responsibilities. She didn't have time to be sick.

She slept in fits and starts until the alarm rang. It went without saying she wouldn't be able to go to work. With only a few shopping days left until Christmas, the department store was in crazy mode. The timing couldn't be worse.

What was that saying? *No good turn goes unpunished.*

Or something like that. Helping Cain and then bragging about showing him kindness had come back to bite her in the butt. And this wasn't a mosquito bite. On no, this felt more like a shark bite.

As soon as she knew she could reach someone at Macy's, Julia phoned in, giving her supervisor the bad news.

"I'm so sorry," she moaned, knowing how the staff supported one another. Her colleagues counted on her. Now they would need to call in a replacement at the very last minute. If she wasn't already sick enough, realizing she was letting everyone down only made her feel worse.

"Don't worry, we'll muddle through." Her supervisor was both kind and understanding, when she could have been upset and angry. "You didn't purposely come down with the flu."

After disconnecting, Julia fought the urge to cry. She was sick and miserable, and it was her own fault. If she'd stayed away from Cain this wouldn't be happening. Instead, she'd had to jump in and save the day like some action hero, never once considering the price she would end up paying.

She'd need to call Jeremy at the Boys and Girls Club and tell him she wouldn't be able to make the practice that evening with the kids. That made her feel even sicker. Jeremy and the kids were counting on her, too.

While she wallowed in self-pity, someone knocked against her front door.

Oh great. The last thing she wanted was company. Dragging the blanket along with her, clenching it closed in a tight fist, she stumbled toward the door.

"Who is it?" She pressed her forehead against the cold wood as a wave of nausea hit her. The entire room started to take a spin.

"Cain," came the response. "Why aren't you at the elevator?"

This was bad. Real bad. "Go away."

She heard his groan from the other side of the door. "No! Julia, do you have the flu?"

"Please, just leave me to my misery."

Her demand was met with silence, and for half a heartbeat she was convinced he'd left. She sighed with relief and started to return to her sofa when he spoke again. She should have known his doing as she asked was too good to be true.

"You said you got a flu shot."

"I did."

"Open up," he demanded.

If he knew how weak she was, he wouldn't be making these demands on her. "I can't."

"Why can't you?"

She wasn't about to admit that she looked like an Ebola patient and didn't want him to see her with her hair sticking out in every direction, wearing no makeup, and still in her pajamas.

"Julia, open the door. Now."

It went without saying her protest would have no sway with him.

"Leave me alone." She knew she sounded overly dramatic, but she couldn't help it.

His response was quick and furious. "Either you open this door or I'm getting the super to open it for me."

"Cain . . ."

"Do it."

"You're going to be late for work," she argued.

"Screw it."

"Please . . ." The word had barely left her mouth when she heard a kick against the door.

He wasn't joking.

Against her better judgment, she unlatched the dead bolt and cracked open the door. "Please, I just want to go back to bed." Although she could see only a sliver of him through the small opening, he looked dressed and ready for work. That should encourage her that whatever bug this was wouldn't last much longer than twenty-four hours.

"Let me in." He gently pushed against the door.

Given no choice, she reluctantly stepped back in order for him to come into her apartment.

She knew she looked dreadful, but watching the way his eyes widened when he saw her punctuated it all the more. The impulse to bury her face in her hands was strong, and she would have if she hadn't needed them to hold up the blanket.

"I'm sorry," he whispered, his voice gentler than she'd ever heard it. "This is my fault. I should never have asked you to stay."

"But I'm glad you did." If she wasn't weak and sick, she'd never have admitted that.

He sighed and slowly shook his head. "I can't bring myself to regret it, either, although I'm sorry you're sick."

Not wanting to look at him, Julia hung her head. "I'll be fine . . . I think. Given time." Suddenly the cup of tea she'd had revolted in her stomach. Dropping the quilt, she raced into the bathroom. Hands braced against the toilet, she lost the tea and whatever else was left in her stomach. Eyes closed, she fervently prayed that when she opened them again Cain would have left the apartment.

God apparently was out Christmas shopping, because He didn't hear her prayer. Carefully straightening, she chanced a look. Sure enough, Cain stood in the doorway to her bathroom with a washcloth in his hand.

"The first twelve hours are the worst."

This was said to encourage her, but it did little to lift her spirits. Groaning, she gratefully accepted the cool cloth and wiped her mouth. "I can't be sick. I've got too much to do today."

"I know the feeling. Come on. I'll tuck you back into bed. Sleep is the best thing you can do for yourself now. I'll check in with you later."

He led her into her bedroom and lifted the covers and then gently covered her up. His hand moved to her forehead and brushed back her hair.

"Do I have a fever?" It certainly felt like she did.

"I don't think so."

That had to be wrong. "I do. I know I do."

"Okay, fine, you have a raging fever."

"That's more like it," she whispered, satisfied now. Sighing, Julia bit into her lower lip. She never expected Cain to be so caring or concerned.

He lingered at her bedside, as if he wanted to do or say something more.

"You don't need to stay with me." She brought her hand out from beneath the blanket and waved him away. "You can go." If he was late for work it would be her fault and she had about all the guilt she could handle for one day.

Even now, she wasn't entirely sure what an actuary did, but it sounded important.

"You'll be all right by yourself?"

"Of course." She wasn't sure, but she didn't want him fussing over her. He was probably right; the best thing for her now was sleep. Although she'd been awake only an hour, her eyes felt heavy.

"Sleep," he whispered.

"Okay." She closed her eyes and it felt good to forget about all she should be doing.

It was then that she felt it. Cain lingered as if he found it hard to leave. And then he did something else. Something that had her heart racing. He leaned down and brushed his lips against her forehead. His touch was so light that for a moment she thought she might have imagined it.

"Sleep tight," Cain said in a low voice, and then he added, "I'll call you later."

She didn't dare speak for fear he'd know she was awake. Only after he left did she remember that Cain couldn't phone her. They'd never exchanged numbers.

It was a few minutes before she heard her apartment door gently close. Within seconds after he left the apartment, Julia was sound asleep.

She woke at about noon and felt only slightly better. The dizziness was gone, although her stomach felt like the bottom of a sewage plant. When she wandered into her kitchen for another cup of tea, she found a note from Cain.

Drink lots of liquids and rest. No arguing.

She rolled her eyes and carted the hot tea to the sofa, where she turned on the television. With cable she had about a hundred different channels to choose from, and she couldn't find a solitary program that interested her. After turning the TV off, she tossed the remote onto the end table. Her phone was there, so she reached for it and checked for messages.

She had several. A couple were from work friends, wishing her a speedy recovery. Cammie had called and left her a voice mail. Julia had been so out of it that she hadn't even heard her phone ring.

There was also a call listed for an unidentified number. She couldn't remember making any calls. She had to wonder if she was in such a fevered state that she'd forgotten. While she held the phone in her hand, it started to buzz. Someone had placed it on vibrate. Checking out the number, she saw it was the same one she'd supposedly called earlier.

"Hello," she answered tentatively.

"You're up."

It was Cain. He'd apparently used her phone to call himself so he had her number.

"Yes."

"You feel better?"

"A little." She laid her head down, as sitting up was making her sick again.

"You sleep?"

"Yeah."

Cain hesitated. "Not very talkative, are you?"

"No." She pressed her head on the sofa pillow and sighed. One would think he'd be grateful.

"First I can't shut you up, and now I can't get you to talk."

Despite his tone, she smiled. "Count your blessings."

He chuckled. "That's my girl."

His girl? He thought of her as his girl. Oh boy, this experiment was getting complicated.

"What time is it?"

"Around one-thirty. I'm on my lunch break."

"Late lunch, isn't it?"

"Later than usual. I had a bunch of work I needed to catch up on."

"Oh."

"You need anything?"

"No. Thanks for calling." She'd been up for less than thirty minutes and already she felt the need to sleep again.

"I'll check in with you later."

"Okay." She was too weak to argue, especially when she knew it was a lost cause, and especially since she looked forward to hearing from him again.

Although she tried to stay awake, Julia slept most of the afternoon. She feared she wouldn't be able to sleep that night and fought it as best she could but quickly succumbed.

She woke to someone at her door.

It could only be Cain.

"Open up, Julia," he called from the other side, confirming her suspicion.

Dragging herself to the door, she turned the lock and stepped back. "It's open."

Cain let himself in, carrying a white paper bag.

"What's that?" If it was food, she wasn't interested.

"Soup."

She held up her hand, disgusted at the mere thought of food. "Take it away. Please."

As she suspected, he ignored her and set the bag on the countertop. "What can I do for you?"

"Give me some privacy."

He chuckled. "If you've got a sassy mouth, that tells me you're feeling better."

"No, I'm not."

"You will soon enough," he promised.

She swayed on her feet, and right away he was at her side, his arm tucked around her waist. His protective action took her by surprise, but no more so than the unexpected thrill she felt being close to Cain. Awareness swept through her and she sucked in a small breath. If he felt anything even close to what she did, he didn't let on, not that she expected he would.

"You okay?" he asked, tightening his hold on her waist.

She nodded rather than respond with words. The truth of it was she wasn't okay. There'd been a physical connection between them that went beyond his gentle touch. Oh my. This shouldn't be happening. Being attracted to him definitely wasn't part of the plan. Her breath came in short spurts until she managed to regulate it again.

His hold loosened, but he didn't release her. "What can I do?"

"Can you help me into the bathroom?"

He didn't answer but carefully steered her down the hallway. Once they were there, he paused and waited before he asked, "Now what?"

"Can you pull the scale out from below the sink?"

"The scale?" he repeated incredulously.

She looked at him, knowing she was pitiful. "I want to weigh myself and see how much weight I've lost."

His look was completely dumbfounded.

"Now kindly leave the room so I can look?"

His eyes rounded to huge saucers. "You have got to be kidding me."

"Just do it," she insisted.

Grumbling, Cain dragged the scale out from where she said it would be and then walked out of the room.

"Don't you dare try and peek, either," she instructed.

She heard him mutter in the hallway outside the door. "Do you honestly think I care about how much you weigh?"

"Cain, please just stay where you are."

"I hope you know you're being absurd." It sounded like he was speaking through clenched teeth.

Julia stiffened, disliking his attitude. "If you're going to get testy with me, you can just go. I want to know how much weight I lost."

He groaned again and she heard him mutter "women" under his breath.

Julia stepped on the scale and swallowed a gasp of surprise. "Five pounds."

"You weigh five pounds?"

"Don't be ridiculous. I lost five pounds."

"Is that good?"

"Of course. It's everything."

He shook his head as if he couldn't believe they were having this conversation. "We done in here?"

"Yup."

Without being asked, he led her back into the living room and helped her onto the sofa. He looked down on her for a moment. "When you feel up to it, eat the soup."

"Okay."

He started toward the door.

"You're leaving?" she blurted out, which only went to show she wasn't thinking on all eight cylinders.

He grinned as if her protest pleased him. "Going to collect Schroeder for a walk. I'll be back."

"Oh good."

His gaze held hers. "That I'm taking the dog for a walk or that I'm coming back?"

"Both," she answered without hesitation.

"I mean what I said about you eating the soup. You're going to eventually need something in your stomach, and as a side benefit it'll make you feel better."

"No, it won't. I'm probably going to die."

He had the audacity to chuckle. "Why doesn't it surprise me that you are such a drama queen?"

"I'm not. I'm sick. I'm suing the company that makes those flu vaccinations. This should never have happened."

Cain laughed as if he found her hilarious.

"Do you enjoy laughing at me?"

"If you remember, you took delight in adding to my misery less than twenty-four hours ago. So yes, this is fun."

"You're coming back soon, right?" Suddenly the thought of being alone depressed her.

"I won't be long."

"Will you watch TV with me?"

"If that's what you want."

"Even if I want to see *Rudolph the Red-Nosed Reindeer*?"

He groaned and nodded. "Even that."

"Thank you."

"You're welcome. Can I leave now?"

"Okay."

As soon as Cain left, Julia reached for her phone and called Cammie.

"Hey," her bestie answered after the first ring. "I wondered when I was going to hear from you."

"I'm in trouble," Julia burst out.

"What kind of trouble? Have you been arrested? Because if so, I know this great lawyer who can get you off the hook."

Cammie's husband was an attorney.

"Not that kind of trouble. Besides, what can David do to help me a thousand miles from Seattle?"

"He'd do whatever was necessary, because he loves me

and he knows you're my best friend. Now tell me what's up."

Julia hardly knew where to start. They spoke nearly every day. If she were to blame anyone, it would be Cammie. This whole experiment had taken control of her life, and Cammie was the one who'd suggested it. Like she told her friend, she was in deep trouble. "First off I've got the flu."

"Oh no."

"And I got it from Cain."

"I read your blog. Do you have any idea how crazy successful this has been? I hope you're looking at the numbers. It's nuts the way people are following what's happening. At this rate you're a shoo-in for the job."

"Yeah, I know. That's where the trouble part comes in."

Her words were met with silence. "Cain found out you're blogging about him?"

"No, thank God." That would be disastrous. "It's worse than that."

"Worse? What's happened?" Cammie demanded.

Julia dragged in a deep breath, hoping that would help her sort through her feelings. "You know how I intensely disliked him not more than a week ago."

"Of course I remember."

"Well . . ." She paused and then blurted it out. "I don't feel that way anymore. In fact, I'm starting to feel the opposite."

Silence.

"Julia." Cammie's voice was low and concerned. "Are you falling for this guy?"

The denial didn't make it past her lips until finally she confessed. "Maybe."

"It's clear I've missed more than a few details in the last couple days. Tell me what's changed."

"It all started this evening when Cain stopped by to check on me. I was shaky on my feet," Julia murmured. "Cain put his arm around me to keep me upright. It was all innocent and . . . and, this is embarrassing to admit, but I wanted more. A lot more."

"What about Cain?"

"I don't know. He's hard to read, but I get the impression he's feeling the same way."

"You're in trouble, all right," Cammie confirmed. "But it's a good kind of trouble. Come on, Julia, it's time you moved on in your life."

Julia flattened her hand against her forehead and it wasn't to check for a temperature. "I know but this complicates everything."

"It does, but you'll figure it all out. Have you . . . you know, told him about the blog?"

"No! Cain is . . . is . . ."

"Is what?"

"I don't know . . . he's Cain. It's complicated."

"Tell me when anything is ever uncomplicated with you," Cammie demanded.

Her friend had a point.

Julia was sick and Cain blamed himself for that. He tried to get her to stay away, but the woman was nothing if not stubborn. The truth was, and it took him time to admit it, he'd been happy to see her. The fact that she'd first brought him the soup and then disinfected his apartment was above and beyond anything he would ever have imagined. She'd even walked Schroeder.

It'd been a long time since he'd felt this strongly attracted to another woman after Dani. His coworker had nearly destroyed his trust; it'd taken him five years to be willing to make himself vulnerable again.

Julia made him want to open his heart, and while he was wary, he felt alive and happy. He found he couldn't wait to see her each morning, wondering what she had up her sleeve.

Even his grandfather had noticed a difference in Cain. He hadn't mentioned Julia, but the old man laughed and said it must be a woman. Cain didn't confirm or deny.

All Cain could say was that life was better than it had been in a good long while.

Julia's Blog

TWELVE DAYS OF CHRISTMAS

December 20

No Good Deed Goes Unpunished

For those of you who suggested I should have drawn a line in the sand when it came to nursing Ebenezer, I want you to know you were right.

Despite getting a flu shot weeks ago, I came down with the same bug and in fact have spent nearly the entire day visiting parts of a toilet that no one should examine that closely.

From the first, I've made no secret of how I feel about my neighbor. I didn't like him when I started this twelve days of kindness. He was annoying. Still is.

He's still unreasonable, too.

And exasperating.

What I didn't expect is that he is also surprisingly caring and thoughtful and funny. Turns out Ebenezer has a sense of humor. Who knew?

When I say caring, I'm not exaggerating. He stopped by this morning and called me twice during the day and then brought me soup. He stayed with me and watched television and didn't even complain about the program I chose.

This morning, he tucked me into bed and kissed my forehead. I know he was probably feeling guilty that I'd gotten the flu, but still . . .

I haven't even told my best friend this—not because I wanted to keep it a secret but because I'm unsure how best to process what's happening.

Tell me, dear readers, what does this mean? What's happening to me? To Ebenezer?

Chapter Eight

Julia felt decidedly better in the morning. Weak as over-cooked pasta but able to function. She didn't dare stay in bed another day, not this close to Christmas. She woke to a text message from Jeremy.

U better?

Much, she replied, balancing the phone on the side of the bathroom sink while she applied her makeup.

Last practice is tomorrow. U OK for that?

I'll be there. Promise.

Thanx. Take care.

Will do.

The holiday program wasn't the last of her volunteer responsibilities, either. She had yet to fulfill her obligation to the Red Bucket Brigade. She'd signed up to ring for an hour and was scheduled for that very afternoon.

Grabbing her phone off the sink, she collected her coat, gloves, and purse and was just about to head out the door when Cain knocked. When she appeared fully dressed and ready for the day, he seemed surprised to see her up and about.

"You're going to work?" he asked.

"I can't stay home," she said, gently attempting to ease her way around him. "People are counting on me."

"I don't think returning to work so soon is a good idea."

"Cain." Her hand moved to his chest. "I don't have time to argue."

"Good." Frowning, as if unsure what to do, he continued to block her way.

"I'm gonna miss my bus," she pleaded. "I'm running late as it is."

To his credit, he moved aside, although reluctantly. The truth was Julia would have enjoyed lounging in bed another day, but it simply wasn't possible. Not with her schedule.

She locked her apartment and met Cain at the elevator. She felt his censure, which she chose to ignore.

"You sure you feel up to this?" he asked.

She did and she didn't, and she answered with a flip-flop of her hand. "I guess we'll see." It was destined to be a long day, and all she could do was hope she had the energy to make it through.

Once inside the elevator, Julia felt Cain exhale in frustration. "I think you should take an extra day. Screw the season."

"Cain, I wish I could, but I can't. You only took off one day, and I'm as tough as you."

He snickered.

"You took a later lunch yesterday because you had so much work to catch up on, right?"

"You're in retail," he countered.

"I still have commitments."

"To sell so many sweaters? Fold display socks?"

Julia stiffened, surprised how offended his comment made her. "If you're belittling my job, I don't appreciate it." Working at Macy's wasn't her choice for a lifelong career, but her years with the company had served her well. She was able to pay her bills until she found employment in her field of work.

He pinched his lips and then sighed. "You're right. That came out wrong. It wasn't what I meant to say. I'm concerned you're going back too soon, and I would hate to see you relapse."

She accepted his apology with a soft smile. "I'll be fine."

"Promise me you'll do your best to take it easy. I have a desk job, but you're going to be on your feet all day."

"I'll do my best," she assured him, touched at his concern.

The elevator doors glided open and they stepped into the lobby. Cain paused long enough to collect his newspaper.

"Hey, is that yours?" she demanded, remembering his habit of stealing. Generally, he collected it earlier when he walked Schroeder.

"Yes," he insisted, without looking.

"Prove it," she demanded, with a hand at her hip. It looked to her like he was up to his old tricks.

Cain grinned. "Aren't you going to be late for your bus?"

"No. Give me that newspaper, I want to check."

"Julia." He groaned and showed her proof positive. His apartment number was marked on the plastic wrapper. "Aren't you going to get yours?" he asked.

"I canceled the newspaper," she said pointedly. "Someone from the building kept stealing it."

Cain laughed out loud, and together they walked out of the building. "You have time for coffee this morning?" he asked.

Watching the approach of the bus, she shook her head. "Not today."

"Tomorrow, then. We'll leave ten minutes early."

Julia did her best to hide a smile as she came to a standstill in front of the bus stop. "Is that a date?"

Walking backward in order to continue their conversation, Cain looked undecided. "Yeah, I guess you could call it that."

"I'm flattered," she called out just before she boarded the bus.

Cain stopped moving and people were forced to walk around him. "Text me and let me know how you're doing today," he called.

"I will if I can." The only time she had to text was her lunch break, and she'd be checking to see what was happening with her blog. Reading the comments and keeping track of the number of hits and shares had become something of an obsession.

"Do it."

"Aye, aye, Captain," she said as she stepped onto the bus. It would have been impossible to hide her smile. Already she felt better, more energized, and she credited Cain.

The driver caught her eye. "You're in good spirits this morning."

Julia realized he was right. "Aren't I every morning?"

"Pretty much; more so than usual today. Looks to me like you got yourself a boyfriend."

Her immediate response was to deny it, but then Julia changed her mind. It would be silly to argue. Still, the bus driver's comment sobered her, and Julia quickly took her seat. Cain was fast becoming someone important in her life, more important than her blog. What had started as an experiment in kindness had turned into something else. Exactly what that "something else" entailed remained an unknown. At this point she was leery of examining it too closely.

By the time Julia took her lunch break, she was physically dragging but on an emotional high. Sitting in the break room, she put her feet up and ate her soup, which seemed the best option for her stomach after her bout with the flu.

Her phone dinged, indicating she had a text message. Even before she went to check, she guessed it was Cain and she was right.

U feeling OK?

Leave it to Cain to be brief and utilitarian. No verbose language for him.

She typed in her reply. Doing fine.

When she didn't get a reply, she set the phone aside but couldn't help feeling disappointed. Her hand was barely off her phone when she snatched it up again, her fingers bouncing against the keys. Looking forward to our date.

Dinner tomorrow night?

If she read that right, Cain was asking her out to dinner. Well, well, that was a big leap from grabbing a cup of coffee in the morning. She loved the idea of having dinner with Cain, but then remembered she had the last practice session with the kids scheduled for the following evening.

Can't. She added a round yellow face with a sad smile.

Y not?

Helping Jeremy. She barely pushed the send button when she got a reply.

Jeremy?

She enjoyed thinking he might be concerned. You jealous?

Should I be?

Depends. It probably wasn't kind, but she didn't think it would hurt to let him assume he wasn't the only man in her life.

Explain tonight.

OK. It'd been childish and immature of her to tease him. What was she thinking? It wasn't like they were in a relationship. They were friends. Nothing more. For that matter, Cain had probably brushed the idea of her being involved with anyone else aside as fictitious. It wasn't like

Julia had a parade of suitors streaming in and out of her apartment. Furthermore, she had no business looking for ways to make Cain jealous.

Because she was caught up in texting with Cain, she barely had time to check her blog results. When she logged on, her eyes felt like they were about to bug out of her head. She'd gotten more than twenty-five thousand hits on her latest post.

Twenty-five thousand.

This was far and beyond anything she'd anticipated when she started this experiment. For the last few days, it hardly felt like being kind to Cain demanded any effort. At first "killing him with kindness" had taken resolve and determination. It didn't seem like he'd ever crack, but in reality it'd taken only a few days, which was astonishing when she thought about it. Even his demeanor had changed. The difference between Cain this morning and the surly, unpleasant guy he'd been as little as a week earlier was night and day.

She read a dozen of the shorter comments from the latest blog, and then, looking at the wall clock, she sighed and returned to the floor.

BetterWatchOut: What does it mean? Sweetie, watch out before your heart gets involved. Or is it too late for that?

MandyPandy: What do you mean no good turn goes unpunished? You got the first real sign this guy is actually human. Ebenezer has a heart and it looks to me like you

just might have found it. Good for you. Keep up the good
work.

When she finished her shift, Julia reported to the volunteer Red Bucket headquarters a block away from Macy's
for her shift at ringing the bell and collecting cash for
those in need. Her commitment was for only an hour,
which was good because of the cold. This wasn't the first
year she'd volunteered, and she had always enjoyed doing
it. People tended to be generous and thoughtful.

The volunteer supervisor gave her directions on where
to report and promised her a replacement would arrive
when her hour was finished. As luck would have it, her assigned position was directly outside of Macy's, which was
sure to be a great spot. While most shoppers wouldn't
know her name, she might look familiar. That gave Julia
hope that those passing by would be inclined to donate.

The retired gentleman she replaced assured her all was
well and this was an excellent location before he handed
over the bell.

"Anything else I should know?" she asked.

"Just be friendly and smile, but a pretty girl like you
shouldn't have a problem filling that bucket. Don't let the
cold get to you. Move your feet often."

"Will do." The sun had long since set and the wind was
piercing. Her predecessor wasn't kidding about the cold.
Julia was glad she'd remembered her gloves but wished
she'd thought to bring the thick cowl her grandmother had
knitted for her last Christmas.

Ringing that little bell for all she was worth, Julia called out in a fun singsong voice, " 'Merry Christmas. God bless us every one.' " She was convinced she'd make Tiny Tim proud.

She could barely contain herself when someone paused long enough to insert a folded one-hundred-dollar bill into the red bucket. "Wow, thank you."

She'd been at her station less than ten minutes when she spied Cain walking toward her. She had accidentally on purpose not mentioned she'd be doing this, fearing he'd have a conniption.

He recognized her at about the same time that she recognized him.

Cain stopped directly in front of her, blocking her exposure to the heavy foot traffic.

"Julia?" He made her name sound like a swear word.

"Cain?" She twisted her body to look past him and continued ringing the bell. "Move. People can't see me."

"What are you doing?" he demanded.

"What does it look like?" she returned. "I'm ringing the bell for charity."

He looked completely exasperated with her. "Do I need to remind you that you just got over the flu?"

Julia couldn't argue. "I couldn't cancel at the last minute. It's hard enough to get volunteers as it is. Now please move. You're discouraging donations."

For half a second it looked like he was about to toss her over his shoulder and gleefully cart her away. Thankfully, he resisted the urge.

"Okay, fine. You want to catch pneumonia, don't let me stop you."

"You aren't going to stop me. Now quit overreacting. I'm only volunteering for an hour."

He shook his head and stalked away down the street, disappearing around the corner and out of view.

Julia's heart sank; the old Cain was back. The one who was impatient, demanding, and impossible. A heaviness settled in her chest and she immediately wanted him to return so she could explain that she was tired and cranky and didn't mean to sound defensive.

Standing just outside of Macy's, shoppers making their way around her, Julia softly sang, ringing the bell in time to the lyrics, doing her best to remain upbeat and energetic and most of all warm. She even joked that people were paying her not to sing.

When she heard Cain's voice come from behind her, she nearly jumped out of her skin. "Here," he said, and held out a Starbucks cup to her. "This should help keep you warm."

"You got me coffee?" Astonished that he would do something so thoughtful, she could barely get the words out.

"Not coffee. A latte. That froufrou drink you like so much."

"My peppermint mocha?" For one wild moment, Julia thought she was going to break into tears of gratitude. "That is so sweet of you." She took a sip and the warmth of it immediately settled into her stomach, chasing away the chill.

He had a Macy's sack in his hand, which he opened, and

brought out a long scarf. "Here, put this on. It will keep your neck warm."

Her lower lip started to quiver then, and she sniffled. "You're being so kind and I was awful to you."

He grinned and looked so wonderful that tears made her vision go blurry.

"You still cold?"

If he'd asked her that earlier, she would have denied it on her deathbed rather than admit she felt half frozen. Right then, lying wasn't an option, and she answered him with a reluctant nod. "I forgot to move my feet and now I can't feel my toes."

Cain stood behind her, leaning in so their bodies aligned and touched. Then he rubbed his hands up and down her arms. It demanded every bit of restraint she could manage not to lean back and let him take her weight. Right away his warmth seeped into her and she relaxed.

"You volunteered for this?" he asked.

"Yes, last month."

An elderly woman stepped up and inserted a bill into the red kettle.

"Thank you," Julia called out after her. "Merry Christmas."

"How much longer do you need to stand here?" Cain asked.

Julia checked her watch. "Not long. Ten minutes or so."

Thankfully, the woman who was due to take her place was five minutes early. Julia relinquished her bell. "This is a great spot," she told her replacement.

Cain continued to hold her close. "Okay, that's it. You're

done for the day." Before she could stop him, he stepped halfway into the street and hailed a taxi. A yellow cab pulled up to the curb and Cain ushered Julia inside.

As soon as she scooted into the car, she was surrounded by warm air, which was pure heaven. Cain climbed in after her. "Do you feel up to a light dinner?"

"Sure."

Cain gave the driver an address she didn't recognize.

"We aren't going to the apartment?" She'd assumed they'd grab something from the deli, which was only a couple blocks from their building, and take it back with them.

"No, this is a place I know. You okay with that?"

"Of course."

"You're not too tired?"

"I'm feeling better now." She was exhausted but unable to refuse herself time with Cain. "You don't need to do this, you know, but I'm glad you are."

"You said you couldn't do dinner tomorrow night."

"I know, I feel bad I can't."

Cain reached for her hand, which was encased in a glove. He intertwined their fingers and stared down. "You're something else."

"I'll take that as a compliment."

The driver pulled up to the curb outside a high-end restaurant, one that had a reputation as being among the best in Seattle. Julia didn't know anyone with the right connections to get a reservation, which rumor claimed required weeks.

Cain seemed to read the surprise in her eyes when she

saw where they were. "The owner is a good friend of mine."

Cain had friends? As soon as the thought passed through her mind, Julia realized how ridiculous she was being. Of course he had friends. Just because she'd never met one didn't mean Cain was an island unto himself. He didn't need to explain that by taking her to meet his friend, she should feel honored. This was a step forward for both of them.

Cain paid for the cab and helped her out. Once inside the restaurant, they were greeted by the hostess and escorted to a plush booth. The hostess pulled the table out, which granted them both easy access to the seat.

"I hope you're hungry enough to appreciate this," Cain said from behind the tall menus.

"Truth is I'm ravenous."

He lowered the menu and smiled at her. "That's my girl."

His girl. This was the second time he'd referred to her that way. The first time it'd unsettled her, but now . . . now she felt a little thrill.

She didn't have time to give much thought to this subtle or not-so-subtle change in Cain, because a man stepped up to the table assessing her, clearly curious. For a second she thought she saw something else, too, although she couldn't be sure she read him correctly. It looked like a warning, perhaps a plea that begged her not to abuse Cain or his heart. She smiled, letting him know without words that she would never do anything to hurt Cain.

Cain made the introductions. "Julia, this is Tom. Tom, Julia."

They exchanged smiles before Tom returned his attention to Cain. "Been awhile since you last brought in a dinner date."

Cain shrugged. "I've been busy."

"He's a stubborn fool, you know," Tom said to Julia. "Stingy, cantankerous, and remote."

Instantly, Julia's hackles rose. "He most certainly is not," she said. She barely knew this friend, but it didn't matter. She wasn't about to let him dis Cain. That very evening Cain had gotten her a scarf. And now that she'd had a good look at the fabric, she saw that it was cashmere, which wasn't cheap. Not only that, Cain had delivered her a hot drink to ensure she stayed warm. And when he thought she wasn't looking, he'd inserted a large bill into the red bucket. "Cain has been thoughtful and generous."

"I did steal your newspaper," Cain reminded her, a smile twitching at the edges of his mouth.

"I've forgiven you for that," she told him, barely able to tear her gaze away to look toward his friend.

Tom's eyes narrowed and he shook his head. "That's low, Cain, taking the poor girl's newspaper. You should be grateful she didn't turn you in to the FBI."

It took Julia a moment to realize Tom was a tease. "You two been friends long?" she asked.

"We were college roommates," Tom explained.

"My bestie was my college roommate, too. Actually, this was her idea," she blurted out, before she realized what she'd said. Right away she wanted to grab back the words.

"What idea?" Cain asked.

"Stuff," she said and swallowed tightly. "All kinds of stuff. Cammie's like that; she's creative and inventive. She's married with a couple kids. Are you married, Tom? What about kids?" She realized she was talking almost nonstop and quickly snapped her mouth closed.

"Married, two kids. Cain is the godfather to the oldest." Tom brought out his phone and showed off family photos.

The waiter stopped by the table and they ordered following Tom's suggestions. He left them alone as soon as the waiter had written down their selections.

No sooner had he stepped away from the booth than two glasses of wine magically appeared. One sip relaxed Julia and she rested her head against the thick cushioned booth.

"I like your friend," she told him. "Has it really been a long time since you brought a woman to dinner here?"

He met her gaze and then looked away. "Five years."

"Why so long?"

"My last experience burned me on relationships. It was a woman from work. I became her advocate at the office and we got close. Apparently, my feelings for her were more serious than hers toward me. She was up for promotion, I recommended her, and once she got the position I was no longer of use to her."

Julia was convinced there was a lot more he wasn't telling her. That he'd been willing to share this much was big, and it helped explain the look his friend had given her.

"She didn't deserve you," Julia said with meaning. "Her loss."

"I enjoyed the way you defended me to Tom," he said, grinning.

She smiled, too. "It took me a minute to realize he's a tease."

"I'm glad you aren't holding it against him." Cain held his wineglass by the stem. "Tom and I are close; he's been with me through a lot and I've been there for him, too."

"It's the same with Cammie and me. I'd like you to meet her one day, and I know she would like to meet you. I don't see her often since she moved to Denver, but we still talk nearly every day."

"She knows about me?"

"A little bit." She feared saying too much.

"What did you tell her?"

This was starting to unsettle her. She'd almost blurted out about the experiment already, and Julia was afraid of what else she might let inadvertently slip. "Just that you're fast becoming a good friend."

Cain reached for her hand, gripping it in his own, and then raised their clenched fists to his mouth, kissing the back of her hand.

"I'm not someone who has a lot of friends. It takes time for me to warm up to people."

"No kidding," Julia joked.

"But once I do, I'm a friend for life."

Her heart melted a little. "I'd like to be your friend," she whispered, and realized she hoped that in time she would be a lot more.

His gaze held hers prisoner. "I think that can be arranged."

Julia was convinced that if they had been someplace other than a busy restaurant Cain would have taken the opportunity to kiss her. And not a peck against her forehead, either. If the look in his eyes was anything to go by, she would have felt that kiss like fire burning through her soul. She wanted that, yearned for it.

Cain must have read the longing in her eyes because he emitted a low groan of warning. "Best not look at me like that while we're in public," he murmured.

Just then their food was delivered and the spell was broken, which in retrospect was a good thing. They lingered over their dinner. Julia told him about dropping out of college midpoint in her junior year.

"I ran out of money and didn't want to spend the rest of my adult life paying student loans." That was the excuse she'd used but it was only the partial truth. She set aside her fork and placed her hand in her lap.

Right away, Cain noticed the change in her. "Julia?"

"I broke up with Dylan my junior year. We'd been dating for nearly three years and I assumed he was the one."

Cain seemed to know this was important. "You loved him?"

"Very much. It wasn't that he cheated on me or that he'd done something unforgivable. We both seemed to realize we weren't right for each other. At the time it seemed the logical thing to do, to go our separate ways. In retrospect, we were right. I thought we were being so mature, and as a matter of fact, we were. What I didn't expect was how hard it would be or how hurt and abandoned I'd feel, even though it was a joint decision. Within a week Dylan was dating someone new and I . . . I floundered, second-guessing myself. It got to be so incredibly painful to see him with another woman that I dropped out of school. It took me six months to make the decision to return. By then Dylan was engaged and I was strong enough emotionally to wish him well."

"And now?"

"Now?"

"Anyone serious since?"

She shook her head. "It's silly, I suppose, but there hasn't been anyone of consequence since."

Reaching for her hand, Cain kissed her fingertips. "Thank you for telling me."

She did her best to put on a happy face and return to her meal. Rarely did she mention Dylan or even think about him any longer. But Cain telling her about his coworker had left the door open for her to share her own disappointments.

By the time they finished, Julia was so exhausted she nearly fell asleep at their table. Cain helped her with her coat, his hands lingering at her shoulders, his breath teasing her ear as he bent down and kissed the side of her neck. Immediate sensation ran down her arms and she shivered.

"It was selfish of me to drag you out when you're just getting over being sick."

"I wouldn't want to have missed this. It was a lovely ending to a very long day. Thank you."

Outside there was a taxi waiting for them, one Tom had ordered.

Cain held open the car door for her and she climbed inside. When he joined her, he wrapped his arm around her shoulders and she rested her head against him and struggled to keep her eyes open. She felt his kiss on the top of her head.

Cocking her head to one side, she studied him and her heart did a little flip-flop. In fact, she couldn't look away. He'd completely mesmerized her. It took her only a moment to realize what was different, and when she did, it felt as if her heart was ready to explode.

The cab dropped them off and they rode the elevator to the third floor in silence. For her part, Julia was caught up in her thoughts and the blog she would write that evening.

Cain walked her to her apartment and hesitated in the hallway. "I had a good time tonight."

She turned to face him, her back to her door. "I did, too. Thank you . . . for everything."

"You're welcome." His voice was rich and low. He didn't seem in any hurry to leave, and she was in no rush to see him go. Slowly he ran his index finger down the side of her face, following the curve of her jaw. His gentle touch felt hot against her skin, and she released a small, incoherent gasp.

If he didn't kiss her soon, she was going to reach for his lapels and jerk him close and do it herself.

Just when she was about to stand on the tips of her toes and kiss him, Cain leaned down and captured her mouth. His kiss was exactly how she'd imagined. Her entire body swayed toward him and he wrapped his arms around her in a hold that half lifted her from the ground.

Julia's arms slipped around his neck as she gave herself over to him. The kiss was intense and deep: a mingling of passion, need, want, desire, and longing. It went on for what seemed like several moments. When they broke apart, they both swayed as if their entire world had made a shift . . . and for Julia it had. This was above and beyond anything she could ever have predicted.

Cain pressed his forehead against hers. "I knew you'd taste like heaven."

His words felt like warm honey.

"You're going to be addictive, aren't you?" he murmured.

"I . . . I don't know . . . maybe . . . I'd like it if I were." With everything in her, she hoped what he said was true.

"One taste will never be enough."

She grazed her lips over his in a near kiss, enjoying the freedom to tease him.

His arms remained around her. Her own were tucked about his waist. "You still going to buy me coffee in the morning?"

"My word is good."

"Mine, too."

Straightening, he kissed the bridge of her nose. "I'll see you in the morning and then you can tell me all about Jeremy."

Julia smiled softly. "In the morning," she promised.

Julia's Blog

TWELVE DAYS OF CHRISTMAS

December 21

The Plot Thickens

There's been a major development. I'm so excited I barely know where to start. I went into this experiment wondering what the effects of kindness would be on my grouchy, no-fun neighbor.

What I never expected, what took me by complete surprise, was how that kindness would be returned. For example, this evening I stood in the cold, volunteering as a bell ringer for the Red Bucket Brigade, when Ebenezer brought me a latte.

But that's just the tip of the iceberg. There's been a major shift in our relationship.

I'm talking seismic.

During my first run-in with Ebenezer, I was caught off guard by his eyes—they were dark and blank. I believe the word I used in talking to a friend was *sinister*. Ebenezer had sinister eyes. It was that very comment that led my friend to suggest I kill him . . . kill him with kindness.

This evening that dark look was gone. It had vaporized completely. When I looked at him, his gaze sparkled with life, with humor, with warmth. At first I doubted myself. Surely I was seeing things. But there was no mistaking what I saw. I'll readily admit it thrilled me. The thing is—and I'm being blatantly honest here—the look in his eyes might have been a reflection of my own.

As a kid I can remember my mother telling me that our lives are merely a reflection of what we see and do. If we are kind, others will treat us with kindness. If we love, we will be loved. If we care, we will be cared for. For a good portion of my life those were just words to me. Good words. Words I wanted to believe.

Now I know they're true.

I've been kind to Ebenezer and now he's kind to me. More than kind. He's been sweet and wonderful. It's my mother's theory of reflection in action. There's far more to this man than I ever expected. Don't be surprised, my friends, but I'm coming to think Ebenezer might be a Prince Charming after all . . .

Chapter Nine

Cain had a difficult time sleeping. His head was full of Julia. It was happening; he could feel it. Despite everything, he was falling for his neighbor and falling hard. It'd been utterly selfish of him to take her to dinner, but he'd wanted—no, needed—more time with her. After working all day and then volunteering, she'd been exhausted. Her tiredness was complicated by the fact that she was coming off the flu. But she had to eat, and Cain suspected she'd skip dinner entirely and he didn't want that to happen.

That was the excuse he'd used to have Tom get them a table. In retrospect, he'd gotten more than he bargained for. Cain tended to be a private person who kept his emotions in check. A woman he'd dated a few times recently insisted he hid himself behind a brick wall. He didn't disagree with her. He was well aware of his tendency to keep his private life private.

What he learned about Julia was that she, too, lived behind a brick wall, only hers was cleverly hidden behind a bright smile and effervescent personality. In the time they'd spent together, and admittedly there hadn't been much, he'd learned relatively little about her life. She'd talked freely about her family and seemed close to her parents and siblings, which was all well and good. What she'd avoided was anything deep, including any reference to previous relationships.

Over dinner she'd opened up to him for the first time and he had with her as well. She hadn't given a lot of detail about what had happened with her college sweetheart, but he could tell the breakup had deeply affected her. By her own admission, she hadn't been in a serious relationship since Dylan.

Cain could appreciate that. He'd been burned himself. Burned badly enough to be leery of women in general, which was one reason he'd been openly suspicious of Julia and her attentions. No one was that happy or friendly without wanting something in return. No one in his experience, anyway. He'd been sure it was all a sick joke. But when he'd asked the barista about her, Cain had been assured this was no act with Julia.

To his credit, Cain had resisted as best he could, but it was as if she were the sun, spreading her glow and warmth over him. Without him ever meaning for it to happen, he found himself caught up in the centrifugal force that was Julia. He'd been swept up by the happiness he felt when he was with her, the feeling of belonging, which was something he hadn't felt in a good long while. It was like an elixir he was fast coming to crave.

His change of heart started when he'd wrongly accused her of stalking him. In retrospect, he'd felt like a bloody fool. When she'd sat down at the piano bench with that choir group he'd nearly groaned out loud. She'd been furious with him and rightly so, but she'd kept her cool. He had to admire the way she'd handled herself.

Later, when he'd come down with the flu, she'd been thoughtful and kind. A smile came when he remembered her marching into his apartment, yellow rubber gloves and bucket in hand. That woman was something else . . .

Cain wasn't much of a Christmas person, never had been. There was only his grandfather and him, and they didn't exchange gifts. For the first time in memory, he was looking forward to Christmas because he had Julia to share the holiday with, and having her in his life made all the difference in the world.

Oh yes, he was falling for her.

Cain fell asleep with a smile on his face.

The entire night Julia felt like she was floating on a dream. She slept deep and woke to her alarm, her heart full of Cain. She could barely wait to see him, barely wait to look into his eyes again, to discover if the spark, that happiness she saw in him, was real and true. If she'd noticed a difference, perhaps his grandfather had as well.

Rushing through her morning ritual, she didn't have

time to check her blog for anything more than statistics. Her readership had grown to numbers that shocked her, doubling almost overnight.

Forty thousand hits and more than a thousand shares. The comments went on for pages. The temptation to stop and read a few of the shorter ones was nearly irresistible. Unfortunately, she had a toothbrush sticking out of the corner of her mouth and didn't have a minute to waste if she was going to meet Cain at the agreed-upon time.

The weather threatened snow, which would be perfect for the season. Wonderful. But snow would make it a nightmare to travel into the heart of the city. Despite what the country seemed to believe regarding the Pacific Northwest, Seattle didn't receive a large amount of snowfall. Maybe once or twice a winter. Being on Puget Sound, temperatures rarely dipped below freezing.

On the off chance there was snow, Julia reached for her knee-high boots. She loved them and had waited until there was a price reduction before she made the purchase. The cashmere scarf Cain bought her was tucked around her neck. This was a special gift she would long treasure, and for more than the quality. Cain had surprised her with his thoughtfulness, making sure she was warm and protected against the elements.

Phil, the barista, greeted Julia and Cain when it came their turn to place an order at Starbucks. He looked from Julia to Cain and then he winked at her. "I see you two have settled your differences."

Cain frowned at the other man. "Can we just get our coffee without the commentary?"

"Cain," she chastised, linking her arm around his. "Be nice."

He continued to glare at the other man. "This is as nice as I get in the mornings."

"Grumble, grumble, grumble," she muttered under her breath, but beneath it all she was smiling.

She claimed a small table while Cain waited for their coffee order to come up. Carrying her latte and his coffee, he joined her a few minutes later, slipping into the chair across from her. His gaze fell on the scarf and she could see he was pleased she was wearing it.

"I heard there's a threat of snow today," she said conversationally as she tasted the peppermint and mocha. It was delicious and exactly the right temperature.

He took a drink from his cup and savored the caffeine before he commented. "What have you got going tonight?"

"Practice with the kids at the Boys and Girls Club." She reminded him they were the reason she couldn't have dinner with him.

He gripped the cup with both hands and held her gaze. "Is Jeremy one of the kids?"

"No, he's the adult leader."

Cain's face tightened. "You and him an item?"

Julia toyed with the idea of purposely making him jealous and quickly decided against it. Cain wouldn't appreciate her sense of humor, especially in the morning. Besides, it would have been childish. "We used to be. These days we're nothing more than friends."

"He feel that way, too?"

"Stop with the inquisition. I dated Jeremy earlier in the year. He's a great guy. He's got a big heart for kids and . . ."

Cain held up his hand, stopping her. "I don't want to listen to a litany of his virtues, Julia."

"Okay." She took another sip of her drink. "Trust me, there's no need to be jealous. It's Christmas and I'm doing him a favor, helping with the kids program and . . ." She paused as an idea came to her.

"And . . . ?" Cain asked.

"Come with me tonight," she blurted out excitedly, warming to the idea. She didn't know why she hadn't thought of this earlier. "I have a couple errands to run after work and I can meet you at the club at seven."

"Why would I want to do that?"

"So you can meet Jeremy, for one. And afterward you can walk me home. Maybe it'll be snowing." That would be perfect. And romantic. She could picture the two of them arm in arm, strolling through the falling snow. The image was enough to make her want to smile and pray for snow, no matter how much of a hassle the aftermath would be.

Cain's head snapped up. "You walk back to the apartment from the club? Alone?"

"It's only a few blocks. The neighborhood's safe."

"A woman alone at night?" He didn't bother to hide his displeasure. "I don't think so."

"Honestly, what is it with you two?" Julia didn't understand it. The club was only a handful of blocks from her apartment, and businesses lined both sides of the street so the entire way was well lit.

"Two? Who else is worrying about you?"

"Jeremy. He doesn't like me walking home alone, either." It might not have been a good idea to mention Jeremy's name again, but if it got Cain to consider coming to the center, then it was worth his darkening frown. "Are you going to meet me or not?"

"I'll be there if for no other reason than to make sure you get home safely."

He didn't sound overly happy about it.

"What time do you think you'll be finished?" he asked.

"Eight or so."

He set his cup down and stood.

Julia followed. Something was wrong, and it was more than the fact that Cain wasn't a morning person. She grabbed hold of his coat sleeve as he started toward the exit. "Cain, what's the matter?"

He went still and his gaze softened when he met her eyes. "What do you mean?"

"You're in a bad mood. Did I do something?"

He stilled. "As a matter of fact, you did."

Her heart raced, fearing that he'd found out about her blog. Eventually she'd need to tell him. She dreaded it and wanted to put it off until after Christmas. Then and only then would she reveal what she'd done and how she'd used him. Until that time she'd pray with every iota of faith she possessed that he wouldn't be offended.

He held her gaze for a long moment. "You want to know what?"

"Yes." It felt as if her heart was in her throat, her pulse pounding in a loud staccato beat, making it hard for her to breathe normally.

"You made me care about you," he admitted.

"Is that a bad thing?" Surely he realized she shared his feelings. She'd come to care about him, too. A lot.

"I promised myself that I wouldn't let that happen again and here I am disliking a man I've never met because I don't want anyone else feeling about you the way I do."

"You don't?" she asked, sighing with the question. He said the most beautiful things and didn't even seem to know it.

He shook his head as if to clear his thoughts. "I don't know what this is, Julia."

"This?"

"Whatever *this* is between us. I have to tell you not only is it unfamiliar, it's unnerving."

Her drink forgotten, Julia watched him closely, her heart in her eyes. It took restraint not to leap up, hurl her arms around his neck, and confess she felt the same way.

"I can't sleep, thinking about you," he said, his voice gruff and impatient. "You were on my mind when I finally went to sleep last night, and then this morning you were the first thing I thought about when the alarm went off. I couldn't wait to see you, to sit and have coffee with you, and I'm already worrying how long it will be until I have a chance to be with you again."

No one had ever said anything more romantic to her, and she pressed her hand over her heart.

"Almost overnight, I find that you've invaded every corner of my well-protected world," he continued. "I don't like it. I don't want to need you and I find that I do and it unsettles me."

"I'm unsettled, too," she told him. "I never thought I'd feel this way, either." Especially about him. Only a few days earlier she'd barely been able to tolerate being in the same elevator with him.

To her disappointment, the bus pulled to a stop out front of Starbucks and she groaned. "I have to go, otherwise I'll be late for work."

"Go," he said impatiently, as if eager to be rid of her, as if sending her on her way would somehow help.

Julia couldn't do it.

"No," she said, making a sudden decision. "I don't care; I'll be late. This is important. You're important."

"Julia, go. It's fine. We'll talk later."

She hesitated and noticed the line at the bus stop was getting short. "I'll go if you kiss me."

He stiffened and shook his head. "Not in this lifetime. I don't do PDAs."

"Just shut up and kiss me," she demanded, grabbing his hand and leading him toward the bus stop.

"Julia . . ."

"Are you going to stand here and argue with me so I miss the bus, am late for work, get fired, and go on welfare?"

He grinned and then his gaze softened as he cupped the side of her face. As if drawn by a will greater than his own, he leaned down and gently pressed his lips over hers. "Satisfied?" he asked as he released her.

"No, but it should be enough to carry me until tonight."

The bus was about to close its doors when she jumped up onto the step, turned, and waved to Cain. "I'll text you later," she called out after him.

Looking disgruntled, he shook his head as if their kiss had punctuated everything he'd just said.

Ten minutes into her lunch break, Julia was too excited to sit still. She grabbed her phone and sent Cain a text. Call me ASAP.

She didn't have long to wait. Her phone rang within seconds of sending him the text.

"What happened?" He sounded breathless, as if he'd raced up three flights of stairs. "Are you okay?"

"Better than okay," she blurted out, clenching her fist against her front. "Oh Cain, the most wonderful, exciting thing has happened and I had to tell you. I didn't mean for you to think anything was wrong, but I couldn't text this, I just couldn't. I needed to hear the sound of your voice."

"Tell me what?"

She needed to tiptoe around this carefully, not revealing too much. She definitely couldn't mention the contest or the blog. "I applied for a social media job, and, Cain, I got a call this morning and I was awarded the position. I'm so excited I could just scream. This is what I've worked so hard for all this time, and now it's a reality."

He chuckled at her joy and excitement. "Congratulations, sweetheart."

Sweetheart?

She froze, her breath trapped in her lungs. "Did you just call me *sweetheart*?"

"Did I?"

He seemed surprised, but she knew it was a ruse.

"You can't say stuff like that over the phone," she told him. "It's against all the laws of love and life."

"What are you talking about?"

"Everyone knows this," she insisted, too happy to care. "It's like this unwritten rule. When you say something romantic and beautiful, it has to be said to the woman when you're face-to-face."

"Am I supposed to apologize now?"

"No, never. What you need to do is say it again, multiple times, but only when we're together. Promise me you will."

"If you insist."

"I'm serious, Cain."

"Okay, fine, I promise. Now go back to the bit about the job. When do you start?"

"Almost right away. I need to give my two weeks' notice and then I should be able to start right after the first of the year. I'm so happy. Do you know how long I've waited for this?" She had Cain to thank, but she couldn't tell him now. Not yet but soon.

"I'm happy for you, baby."

OMG. "There, you did it again. You called me *baby*. Stop, please stop; otherwise, I might do something really foolish, like cry or shout or act completely out of character. A person can only hold so much happiness inside them at a time."

"If I was with you now I'd kiss you senseless."

"You would?" It felt as if her heart was melting; her knees were already weak. She hadn't been kidding when she said she could only take so much happiness at a time.

"You have no idea, do you?"

She could tell he was serious by the timbre of his voice.

"Yeah," she answered, sobering herself. "I think I do." Cain was simply stating the very things she was feeling. She could barely wait for that evening when she saw him.

"Be ready tonight," she said. "I'm going to make you say everything all over again. You must. It's required in order to right the universe."

"Then, by all means, we can't have the universe spinning out of control."

Julia didn't know if she could wait that long. "Maybe you could meet me at Manor House."

Oops, that was a mistake. He wasn't supposed to know that she'd been secretly visiting his grandfather.

"Manor House? What are you doing there? Is there another concert?"

Exhaling a deep breath, Julia sat down and leaned forward, pressing her elbows against her knees. "No. I . . . I have a small confession to make."

"Julia . . . ?" The hesitation in his voice rocked her.

"It's nothing bad, I promise."

"Let me be the judge of that."

She squeezed her eyes closed. "I met your grandfather."

Her words were followed with a hollow silence. She counted to twenty before Cain spoke again.

"When did you meet Bernie?"

She might as well ease him into the truth. "Shortly after the concert."

"How?"

"Can we talk about this later?"

"No."

"All right, full confession: I saw the two of you together at the concert and I figured you must be related, so I went to visit him. Actually, I've been to see him twice."

"Why?"

How she wished he'd do more than ask her one-word questions. "Are you angry?"

He repeated the question. "Why?"

"Because I wanted to know more about you. Bernie's great. I brought him the cookies you refused. He claimed they were his favorite, but I think I could have baked just about any kind and it would have been his favorite."

"You bribed him with cookies?"

"*Bribe* might be too strong a word." She cleared her throat when she realized her voice had dropped to little more than a whisper. "We played cribbage. You have a wonderful grandfather; I like him, Cain. We were going to surprise you, but I guess I ruined that."

"You invited him to have Christmas dinner with you, didn't you?"

"Yes. You're included."

"That was the surprise he's been teasing me about. You're the surprise?"

"Yup. That would be me," she said, raising her voice an entire octave.

"Now you're telling me visiting Bernie was the errand you had to run after work?"

She was surprised he remembered her mentioning that. "Yes."

"He's quite taken with you."

"Your grandfather told you about me?" Apparently, she wasn't the only one keeping secrets.

"Not specifically. Bernie said he met a lady friend who invited him to Christmas dinner. Didn't include me. He was adamant I should find my own sweetheart."

"And you did, and before you argue, there's no reneging because you've already called me your sweetheart once today. You can't take it back. I won't let you."

"I won't renege."

"Good. Please don't be upset with me."

"Going behind my back doesn't sit well with me, Julia, but I'm willing to let this slide, seeing that you've won over my grandfather."

"Did I win you over, too?" she asked in low tones.

"We'll discuss that tonight. I'll see you at eight at the Boys and Girls Club and we can discuss this when I walk you home."

"Okay." She happened to catch a glimpse of her watch. "Oh no, my lunch break is over. I've got to get back on the floor." She hated the conversation to end. Hearing Cain's voice, telling him her good news, would need to be enough until she caught up with him later.

Earlier he'd complained about the depth and strength of the development of their relationship. It pained him to let her know that she'd become important to him. What Cain didn't realize was the depth of her own feelings. No one was more surprised with how well this challenge had gone than Julia.

Bernie was waiting for her when she arrived later that evening. He sat in the same room where the church group had sung and brightened the instant he saw her.

"So you told him?" he said, grinning broadly when she took the chair next to him.

"It slipped out. He called you?"

"Oh yes. Wanted to know exactly what I'd told you. Don't think Cain's happy with either one of us, but don't you worry your pretty face, he'll get over it."

Her shoulders relaxed. She'd been fairly certain Cain would contact his grandfather.

"You've made a big difference in his life in the last week or so," Bernie said, grinning and looking pleased. "Hard to believe the change in that boy."

Julia had almost forgotten the reason she'd scheduled this visit. "Oh, I'm so glad you said something. When was the last time you saw Cain?"

"Tuesday. He joins me for lunch on Tuesdays."

"Did you notice anything different about him?" she asked.

"How'd you mean? He mentioned you, which surprised me. I told him I had a hot date for Christmas dinner and he should find his own woman because I wasn't sharing."

She laughed before a small thrill went through her. "Cain mentioned me? What did he say?"

Bernie grinned, looking almost boyish. "Just that there was this woman in his apartment complex who was driving him nuts, wouldn't leave him alone. I went along with it, pretended I didn't know it was you. I asked him if he'd reported this woman to the police for hassling him."

Julia gasped. "You didn't!"

"I sure did, and then Cain told me this troublesome woman had wormed her way into his life and she wasn't nearly as irritating as he first thought."

Hearing this, Julia relaxed. "That's good to hear."

"Now, what was it you expected me to notice different about my grandson?"

"His eyes," Julia told him. "When we first met they were blank, indifferent, and, oh, I don't know, emotionless, I guess. Then last night I noticed a light in them, a spark, and it excited me. It made me wonder if you'd seen the same thing."

Bernie pinched his nose, as if trying to conjure up his grandson's look the last time Cain had visited. "Now that you mention it, I think that maybe I did notice a change."

"You did?" Bernie had no idea how much hearing that thrilled her.

"I detected a difference right off but wasn't able to put my finger on it. He's joining us for Christmas?"

"Yes. He might not know it yet, but he'll be there, if I have to drag him out of his apartment and across the hall."

"I doubt my grandson will be fighting you. You got him, Julia. Hook, line, and sinker. That boy is completely taken with you. Been a long time since I've seen that much life in him. He's not one to show how he feels about things.

Never has been. Even when that girl from his office used him, he barely said a word. It wasn't until afterward that I was able to connect the dots and realize how badly he'd been burned."

"I'll never hurt him."

"I know you won't."

All Julia could do was hope and pray that was the case once Cain learned about the blog.

Julia stayed and visited with Bernie until it was time for him to join his friends in the dining room for dinner. With time to kill, she pulled out her laptop and started reading comments, but there were just too many.

She had more than a hundred thousand hits, and people were eager for an update. Wanting to keep the interest from waning, she decided not to wait until she got home to write her next post.

Pulling up a blank page, her fingers flew across the keyboard. She had a lot to report. A lot to say.

Julia's Blog

TWELVE DAYS OF CHRISTMAS

December 22

An Observation

When I started this project, I never thought to look up the meaning of the word *kindness* in the dictionary. I figured I knew a lot about the act of being kind, and what I didn't know I'd play by ear.

I was wrong. I knew very little.

Being kind is like looking at your own reflection in the calm waters of a lake. Then the act of kindness ripples those waters, like a stone tossed upon the surface. Whoa, I'm getting all introspective and I don't mean to be. My point is that the first few days of this experiment, I gritted my teeth as I bent over backward to be kind to the very unlikable Ebenezer. Despite my efforts, he made it difficult. Thanks to the encouragement from you, my readers, I persisted.

In an amazingly short amount of time, Ebenezer has

come to show real kindness to me. This evening he'll be walking me home from a Christmas rehearsal. This is the same man who thoughtlessly took my newspaper and cringed like he'd tasted something foul when I greeted him in the mornings. The very same person.

The difference has been kindness.

It's that reflection thing I mentioned previously. I was kind to Ebenezer and then he was kind to me—the rippling effect. Truthfully, when I started this, I didn't know what to expect. I figured at the end of the Twelve Days of Christmas I'd be lucky if he was willing to talk to me.

From what I've seen, he doesn't feel I'm an irritation any longer, and my feelings for him have changed, too. This afternoon, he used a term of endearment when referring to me. He admitted he doesn't want to care about me. But he does. He cares.

And we all know why. It boils down to that single word.

Several of you have written to tell me you're doing your own experiments in kindness. Some with more success than others. For those of you who aren't seeing any difference, don't give up. I'm so happy this idea has caught on. Excited to be part of it. Thrilled to report my progress.

Ebenezer and I are meeting up again shortly when he walks me home. I'm anxious to see him, to laugh with him, and for him to call me "sweetheart."

Until tomorrow, dear readers.

Chapter Ten

"Jeremy, the kids sound great." Julia couldn't be happier with how well the practice session had gone. "Missing the one day didn't hurt us a bit."

Looking pleased himself, Jeremy leaned against the piano. "I think so, too. We're as ready as we'll ever be for the program tomorrow night."

Julia was delighted. She loved watching the children perform. They were excited to perform for their families and friends and had worked hard to learn the words and the melodies. It made her role accompanying them on the piano ten times easier. As she watched their eager young faces, it made her long for a family of her own one day.

Immediately, she thought of Cain. While it was early in their relationship, way early, she had a good feeling about the two of them. The attraction between them intensified each and every day in ways it never had in previous—albeit short-lived—relationships.

Admittedly, it was too soon to be thinking of anything permanent. Yet they were building a solid foundation, and that pleased her.

That foundation would be far less stable once he learned about her blog. A sense of apprehension filled her. Fearing he might be upset, Julia had realized she needed to tell Cain what she'd been doing. However, she didn't think it would go well if she unloaded it all on him at once, so she'd decided to explain it in stages.

The slip of the tongue when she'd confessed she'd connected with his grandfather had been a blessing. Now that Cain knew she'd sought out Bernie, it'd opened the door for the full disclosure.

Jeremy's phone beeped, indicating he had a message. He unclipped the phone from his belt, read it, and looked up at her. "Do you know a man by the name of Cain Maddox?"

Julia immediately brightened. "Yes. Is he here?"

"Yes. That was Louis. Your friend arrived about forty minutes ago. He and Louis are apparently talking basketball."

Julia had no idea Cain was keen on the sport, but then there was plenty she didn't know about him yet.

"Louis said this guy is waiting for you."

"That's great." Julia knew Louis worked with the boys in the gym.

She noticed Jeremy was closely studying her and he

didn't look pleased. "Would you like to meet Cain?" she asked.

He shrugged, not revealing a lot of enthusiasm. "I guess."

They met up with Cain and Louis in the gym, and when Cain saw her, he ended his conversation and started walking toward her. Julia's heart beat a bit faster when she noticed Cain's look. It was as if she were the focal point of his entire world. The gym could have caved in around them and she doubted that he would have noticed. She was all he saw and he was all she saw. They met in the middle and still didn't look away from each other.

"I don't like the idea of you walking alone back to the apartment," Jeremy was saying.

Cain snapped his eyes away from Julia.

"I'll get my coat and walk you back," Jeremy said, ignoring Cain.

"I'll walk Julia home," Cain said, moving so he stood directly in front of Jeremy.

The two men were toe to toe, eye to eye. The tension between them was tight, vibrating with antagonism.

"I'm happy to do it," Jeremy insisted.

"Not happening" was Cain's response.

"Cain?"

He ignored her when she touched his sleeve.

She'd been sure Jeremy wasn't interested in her. Now this. Cain wasn't behaving any better, either.

"Boys, stop!" Julia said, because that was exactly the way they were acting—like schoolboys on the playground. It felt like the entire room went silent, although that wasn't the case. The casual game of basketball was taking place behind them, but for all the attention Cain and Jeremy gave it they might as well have been squaring off in a dark alley.

"Cain, this is Jeremy," she said, hoping to lessen the tension between the two men. "Jeremy, Cain."

Neither blinked.

Julia was stunned. She'd never seen Jeremy act territorial before, and for that matter, she hadn't seen this side of Cain, either. Jeremy and Julia weren't an item and in reality had never been. They were friends. Good friends who had gone out on a couple dates. He'd asked a favor of her and she was happy to accompany the children for the holiday program. What she saw in him now was completely out of character and unprecedented.

Neither man was backing down.

"Listen, you two, I am not a fire hydrant and this isn't a pissing contest."

If they were going to behave like Neanderthals, she wasn't going to stick around and watch. She already had her coat and purse with her. While the two continued their stare-off, she slipped on her thick jacket, buttoned it up, and swung her purse over her shoulder.

"See you both tomorrow." With that said, Julia walked out of the gym and found her way to the exit. The cold wind slapped her in the face once she was outside. The threat of snow hung in the air. So much for the romantic picture of walking home hand in hand with Cain.

Hunching her shoulders against the cold, she'd walked

little more than a block when she heard Cain calling her name. She didn't stop.

"Julia, slow down."

She did, but she wasn't happy. He eventually caught up with her and matched his steps to hers.

"What was that about?" she demanded, not giving him a chance to speak.

He answered with a question of his own. "I thought you said you and Jeremy were just friends."

"We are."

Cain snickered. "I don't think he got the memo."

"Of course he did. We haven't dated in months."

"He's still interested in you."

Julia rolled her eyes. "Don't be ridiculous."

"Were you not in that gym?" Cain demanded. "The minute he walked into the room, his eyes were laser points drilling me. He's hung up on you and he didn't hesitate to let me know."

"You're imagining things."

"Don't give me that. You saw the way he reacted."

"I saw the way you reacted," she accused. "It was completely asinine."

Cain came to a sudden halt. "Listen, I'm not a mind reader. If you have feelings for this guy and are using me to make him jealous, then . . ."

Julia gasped. "Are you seriously asking me that? I already told you there's nothing romantic between Jeremy and me. Nothing. If he's harboring feelings, then it's news to me. For you to even suggest I would use you says how little you know me." Not waiting for his reaction, she started walking again, increasing her pace, doing her best to control her irritation.

Cain joined her, matching his footsteps to hers. "Okay, you're right, I shouldn't have suggested you would use me. Someone else did once, so I'm sensitive to it."

Julia felt her stomach lurch because she was using him, just not the way he implied.

"Did you hear me?" he demanded.

"Yes, I heard you."

"Do you understand what I'm saying?"

She glanced over at him. "Apparently not. You'd better explain it to me."

He paused and reached for her, taking her gently by the shoulders and turning her so that they were face-to-face. "I'm walking you home, and it isn't because I live in the same apartment building as you. It's because Jeremy needed to know I wasn't backing down. If he wants you, then too bad. It's not happening."

"I am not a piece of property for the two of you to fight over."

"No, you're not," he agreed. "You're important to me and I'm not letting you go without making sure it's what you want. If that means staring down or having words with your *friend,* then so be it." His gaze bored into hers, waiting.

"You matter to me, too," she whispered. Right away she could see he wanted more, needed more. "You're the one I dream about at night, the one I look forward to seeing in the mornings, the one who makes my heart sing with joy. If that isn't enough, then I don't know what else I can say."

For the first time since they started walking, Cain grinned. His shoulders visibly relaxed. "It's enough." He wrapped his arms around her waist and pulled her close to his side. "So did you go see my grandfather?"

"You called and talked to him."

"He told you, did he?"

"Yup."

"You're a sneaky woman, Julia Padden."

Now was as good a time as any to fill him in a bit more on what she'd been doing. "Can we stop at Starbucks for a few minutes?" Neutral territory would work best for what she had to say. If Cain got upset with her, he wasn't likely to make a scene in a public place.

Like before, she found them a table while Cain ordered their drinks. He returned in only a few minutes, as she didn't want anything more than coffee. Cain sat down across from her and handed her the hot coffee. Her hands went around the cup, the warmth seeping up her arms.

"Julia?" Cain's voice was full of uncertainty when he read the reluctance in her.

She briefly looked up and offered him a weak smile. "I have something to tell you that you might not like. I'd rather get it out in the open now." Her heart raced at an alarming rate.

"Okay."

The hesitation she heard in him wasn't helping.

"Are you married?" he asked.

She snapped her head up to look at him. "Married? Me? No."

"Do you want to be?"

"Yes, of course, someday." She wasn't sure where these questions were leading. "Actually, working with those kids at the center has made me think more about wanting a family of my own one day."

"They're great, aren't they?"

"The best."

"Okay, so what you want to tell me isn't the fact that you're married."

"No, no, it's nothing like that."

He looked relieved, which made her wonder if maybe that old girlfriend from his office had lied about more than her intentions.

"What's got you so twisted up in knots that you're having a hard time spitting it out?"

Drawing in a deep breath, hoping that would calm her heart, Julia looked up and met his gaze. "Would you mind holding my hand?" she asked.

He reached across the table and gripped her hand.

"You remember the morning I found you stealing my newspaper?"

He grinned as if the memory was a fond one. "I'm not likely to forget it. Your eyes were snapping fire at me."

"I was upset."

His eyes softened. "You have a hard time hiding the way you feel, Julia. You should never play poker."

He was right, which made what she had to say all the more complex. "I mentioned Cammie, my college roommate, remember?"

He nodded.

Her fingers grabbed hold of his, needing the reassurance of his touch.

"When I told Cammie what you'd done, she suggested I kill you."

Cain's eyes widened.

". . . with kindness." She held his look, waiting for his reaction. He didn't betray any of what he was thinking, which made her all the more nervous.

It took a moment for him to understand what she'd said. "That's why you decided to deliver my newspaper to my door?"

She answered with an awkward smile. "Yup. It was a test of sorts to see if kindness made a difference in the way you treated me."

He ignored her explanation. "And the cookies?"

"And the cookies," she echoed.

His face tightened. "So you looked upon me as a challenge."

This was the hard part. "Yes, in the beginning, but you aren't any longer."

"What am I now?" he asked, releasing her hand. He sat up straighter and leaned back as if physically and emotionally separating himself from her.

Julia knew her answer would determine the outcome of their relationship. "You're so much more than a challenge. When I'm with you I feel everything more intensely. The sun is brighter, the sky is bluer. My thoughts revolve around you. The experiment was to see if kindness would make a difference, and, Cain, can't you see that it has? In the beginning I didn't like you. I thought you were . . .

well, it doesn't matter, because I don't think that way any longer." She chanced looking at him, but he remained stiff and unreadable. "I don't know which one of us changed. If it was you or me or both of us at the same time, I can't say. All I know for sure, after the transformation took place, I wouldn't change a minute of my time with you since this started. Not a single minute."

"What about the flu? You'd want to go through that again?"

"Yes, even the flu, because it was a turning point for us."

He exhaled. "You're basically telling me this has all been a game."

"Not a game. Come on, Cain, admit it. You didn't like me, either. If you recall, you found my morning chatter to be an annoyance. And you thought I was stalking you, so no fair, you can't get all righteous on me."

"I'm not."

She thought she saw the beginning of a smile. "Yes, you are. You weren't any more interested in knowing me than I was in becoming friends with you. We both changed, and for that I'll forever be grateful."

"I'm not so bad, you know."

"You can be."

"So can you."

She couldn't argue.

His look sobered. "I need to think on this."

"Okay." She didn't blame him. If their roles had been reversed, she might easily feel the same.

"I need to be in the office early tomorrow so I won't see you in the morning."

Disappointment settled over her and she lowered her gaze, not wanting him to notice her reaction. "Okay."

He started to get up and took his coffee with him. He hadn't suggested they see each other again, and that worried her.

"The program is tomorrow evening," she said, standing now, too. It was her way of asking if he would attend. She hoped he would.

"So I heard."

"Will you come?"

He hesitated as if weighing the decision. "I have to think."

"About attending?" she asked.

He shook his head. "Yes, but it's more than that. I appreciate you telling me, but I'm going to need time to process this."

She swallowed hard. If he felt strongly about this, then she could only imagine what his reaction would be when he learned about her blog. This didn't bode well.

He was silent on the short walk back to the apartment and in the elevator ride to the third floor. They parted ways at their respective doors.

Cain's back was to her and she watched as he inserted his key.

"Cain?"

He looked over his shoulder.

"Before you go inside, would you mind hugging me?"

For just an instant she thought he was about to turn her down. After the slightest hesitation, he covered the space that separated them and gathered her in his arms, squeezing her tightly against him. Julia rubbed her nose against his neck.

"What are you doing?" he asked.

"Smelling you."

"What?"

"I'm smelling you in case you decide you don't want anything more to do with me, in which case I want to remember your scent."

He loosened his grip. "You're a strange woman."

"Yeah, maybe I am."

Julia had a hard time sleeping that night. She woke in the wee hours of the morning and logged on to her computer. Because she'd posted her blog earlier, she set about reading the comments. Several had been following her blog almost from the beginning and she'd come to automatically look for their names.

SantaGirl: Whoa, Nellie. I hope you're listening to yourself. You've gone soft, girlie. This guy is getting to you. Not that it's a bad thing. Just take care. Are you sure you want to involve your heart, especially if Ebenezer hasn't got a clue what you're doing?

Good question. Julia was looking to rectify that, though.

Then she read a comment that caused her to gasp out loud. It was from Sheila Coan, a news reporter at a local Seattle television station. Julia recognized the name.

TVGirl: Surprised to learn you're from the area. Would love to interview you and Ebenezer. Think it would be a great human interest story for Christmas Eve. Perfect, really. Give the station a call at 209–555–1007, tell them who you are, and they'll connect you with me. We'll set a time and place.

Julia's heart slammed against her chest so hard she was afraid she was about to crack a rib. She didn't know how the reporter was able to learn where she lived. She didn't believe she'd given any indication of her location. Maybe she had without knowing it. Not that it mattered. She wasn't about to give the woman an interview.

Julia immediately responded to the email address rather than contacting the reporter personally and denied the request. An interview with Cain? Julia couldn't think of anything worse. Letting him know about the blog would ruin everything if their relationship wasn't already down the toilet with the half-truth she'd admitted to.

Her morning seemed empty and dull without seeing Cain. It felt odd, as if she had forgotten something important, like her purse or her coat. Riding on the bus, she leaned her head against the window as a brooding sense of worry filled her.

Cain had been upset even knowing she'd set out to trip him up with kindness. If he couldn't deal with that, then the blog would send him completely over the edge. And he'd eventually find out about it. That was inevitable. Inhaling, she decided the only thing to do was cross that bridge when necessary. For now, they had to find a way to get over the first hurdle.

If Cain showed up for the program at the Boys and Girls Club, she'd know he was willing to move ahead. Cain knew the program was important to her. She'd basically asked him to attend. If he ignored her request, it would tell her everything.

With only a few shopping days left until Christmas, Macy's was crazy busy. As soon as her shift ended, Julia rushed from the department store to the Boys and Girls Club. By the time she arrived, the auditorium had already started to fill up with family and friends.

Scanning the area, Julia didn't see Cain. She did her best to swallow her disappointment. Her heart felt as if it was loaded down with weights.

Jeremy trapped her into a conversation the minute she showed up. It was as if he'd been waiting for her arrival all day. When he spoke, his tone was demanding and sharp. "Who was that guy from last night?"

Julia ignored him and slid onto the piano bench.

"You never mentioned him before."

Irritated with her friend, she looked up from the piano keys. "Cain's my neighbor."

"You two are dating?"

She wasn't sure what to say and decided to think positively. "You could say that."

"You should have let me know." Jeremy eyes were full of accusation.

"Why would I do that?" she flared back, not wanting to

get into this now, and not with him. "I don't know where this is coming from with you, Jeremy. We went out a few times, that's all."

The announcer stepped forward and the room slowly went silent as the excited voices faded to a low hum and then nothing.

Julia could see Jeremy wanted to say more, but now definitely wasn't the time. After a few words of introduction from the head of the Boys and Girls Club, the children filed onto the stage one by one, their faces alight with huge smiles. They stood at attention and faced the audience. Julia set her hands on the keyboard and started to play.

The Christmas program was a huge success. Julia would have felt a hundred times better if Cain had made a showing. But she didn't see him and her heart felt heavy in her chest, weighted down with disappointment and regret. At the end of the evening, while Julia gathered up her things, Jeremy approached her.

"We didn't finish our conversation."

"We did," she insisted. "Really, Jeremy, there isn't anything more to say."

He looked as if he was ready to argue and then seemed to change his mind. "Everyone appreciates your help with the program tonight."

"I was happy to do it." She was glad to be able to contribute in a small way to the enjoyment of Christmas for these children.

Julia collected her coat and purse and headed for the door with Jeremy following on her heels.

"I'll walk you home," he said, reaching for his own coat.

Stepping out of the shadows, Cain spoke up. "I'm going that way. I'll walk Julia home."

"Cain." Julia was so happy to see him that she flew into his embrace, hugging him so close it was a wonder he could manage to breathe.

Automatically, his arms wrapped around her. He kissed the top of her head and rubbed his chin over her crown. "You ready to head home?" he asked.

She nodded and smiled at Jeremy. "Thanks for the offer, but Cain is here."

Jeremy looked from one to the other and then nodded with acceptance. He got the point. "See ya, Julia."

"Merry Christmas."

Raising his hand, Jeremy looked at Cain with what could only be described as resignation. "To you, too." He left them alone.

Julia waited until they were outside to speak. "I didn't see you."

"I was delayed at the office and didn't get here until the program was half over."

She turned and buried her head against his chest. "I worried all day. I was afraid if you stayed away tonight it was over for us. I figured this was your way of telling me you'd decided you wanted nothing more to do with me."

"I don't like what you did."

"I know." Heaven help her when he learned the rest of it.

"But I gave it a good deal of thought and I can't argue with the outcome."

"Me neither." She looked up at him, her heart in her eyes. "Can we put it behind us and move forward?"

Cain's gaze softened as he looked down at her. "I don't know, Julia. I'd accepted my life and was comfortable. I was content and then you plowed your way into my world and turned it upside down."

"You aren't content any longer?"

"No. I'm finding I want more. I'm not sure that's a good thing and you're to blame."

"But it is good for both of us, Cain."

"I think it just might be," he whispered before leaning down and pressing his lips to hers in a kiss that seemed an absolution and a new beginning.

Julia opened to him, letting him know in a single kiss how important he was to her and at the same time praying he would never learn about her blog.

Julia's Blog

TWELVE DAYS OF CHRISTMAS

December 23

A Small Bump in the Road

There's been a bit of trouble in paradise since I posted my blog yesterday.

Isn't that the way life goes? Just when everything seems perfect and nothing could possibly go wrong, then, boom, you're tossed onto your butt, wondering what in the name of heaven happened.

I told Ebenezer about the experiment.

I have not told him about this blog, and once he finds out I fear it'll be the nail in the coffin of our relationship. I don't know that I can bear for that to happen. If you've followed me this far, you've surely seen the changes in Ebenezer and, just as important, the changes in me.

I'm planning to keep my blog a secret from him for a while longer, but this is a decision I fear I can't make on my own. So once more I'm turning to you, my faithful readers. I need your advice.

Do I tell him? If so, when?

Or do I leave the whole thing to chance?

Ebenezer might go years and never find out what I've done.

We just leapt over one hurdle, and presenting another so soon after might be too much.

I'm convinced it would be, and at the same time I don't know that I can hide this. It's against my nature to be deceitful. Or more deceitful than I've already been.

I hate this. Ebenezer has been hurt before, and if he learns what I've been doing he might never trust me again. And I don't know that I could bear hurting him.

So tell what would be best.

I need your help now more than ever.

Chapter Eleven

Julia's phone rang ten minutes before she headed out the door to shop for Christmas dinner with Bernie and Cain. Caller ID told her it was Cammie, so she grabbed it.

"Merry Christmas Eve," her best friend greeted.

"Merry Christmas Eve to you, too," Julia echoed.

"You working today?"

"No, I'm one of the fortunate few." She'd worked Black Friday in the wee hours of the morning in exchange for having Christmas Eve off. It'd been a fair trade. She had only a handful of items to pick up for Christmas dinner and she was up and about early.

She'd decided on the traditional turkey dinner with all the fixings. She'd already connected with her mother for instructions twice for the simple reason she was determined to make this the best meal possible and every bit as good as what she remembered from her childhood. There were a couple of other dishes she wanted to try, too. Julia could read a recipe book like it was a bestselling novel. Having guests made the holiday all the more special. Friends from work had invited her to join them as they had in the past, but this year she had the opportunity to welcome her own guests.

"What's up?"

"I read your blog this morning and comments from the day before. Did you see the request that came from that reporter? How'd she know you were in Seattle?"

"I wondered that, too. Going back before I started the kindness blog, I wrote one about riding the bus in downtown Seattle on my way to work. Not my most brilliant post."

"Wow, she had to dig to see that. You going to give her the interview?"

Her heart clenched with anxiety. "I wrote back and told her no way."

"That might not be good enough."

Fear knifed through Julia like a hot blade through butter. "What do you mean?"

"This reporter might be able to track you down."

That couldn't happen, it just couldn't. While pressing the phone to her ear, Julia reached for her coat, struggling to get her arm in the sleeve and still continue their conversation.

"If I were you, I wouldn't leave it to chance," Cammie advised. "Tell Cain."

"I can't." She switched the phone to the other side of her head as she struggled with the second sleeve.

"Tell him," Cammie repeated. "Before he finds out from someone else. You haven't given a lot of detail in your posts, but I know you, I've read between the lines. You're really into this guy, Julia, unlike anyone else you've dated since Dylan. Don't risk ruining this when obviously this relationship is important to you."

Cammie was wise beyond her years. "Okay, okay, you're right, but after Christmas. I need to get through Christmas first."

"Don't put it off any longer than that. If you do, you'll regret it. Cain needs to know."

"You're right. I know you're right. I won't put it off," Julia promised.

"Call me after you've had the talk."

"I will." They ended the conversation, and Julia tossed her phone in her purse and headed out the door.

Cain had the day off and she was grateful. They'd get through Christmas and she'd have a heart-to-heart with him, carefully planning what she had to say. She'd need to prep him first, let him know how important he was to her. It was vital that he understand she'd never use him for her own selfish purposes. Explaining that would be the most difficult part. All she could do was pray Cain would be willing to listen.

When the elevator landed on the ground floor, Julia stepped out and nearly stumbled over a cameraman and a reporter with a mike in her hand.

Julia froze. Literally froze. She couldn't breathe, couldn't move.

"Are you Julia Padden?" The familiar face of Sheila Coan loomed in front of her.

If she'd had half a brain she would have denied it and forced her way out the door. Instead, she stood like a deer caught in the headlights. Only it was a freight train that had lost its brakes and was careering toward her. She could see it coming and was powerless to move.

"I'm here about your blog. Congratulations on the success of 'Twelve Days of Christmas'! I have to say, after reading your posts, I wouldn't mind meeting Ebenezer myself." Thankfully, she kept the microphone lowered to her side. The cameraman removed the camera from his shoulder as well, waiting for the reporter's cue to start filming.

"How . . . how did you find me?" Julia asked, once she gathered her wits about her.

Sheila grinned and looked pleased with herself. "A reporter has her ways."

"Oh."

"The blog has captured a lot of attention with the power of kindness trending around the country."

"Yes, but . . ."

"Tell me about Ebenezer."

"No." Julia adamantly shook her head. No way was Julia chancing Cain learning about this. "I believe I already told you I'm not interested in giving you an interview."

"Yes, I got your reply, but the story is such a good one

and I know our viewers would benefit from what you learned. I'm hoping you'll reconsider."

"No, please, just go." The attention she was getting from her neighbors and those in the foyer was highly embarrassing.

Sheila Coan didn't bother to hide her disappointment. She handed Julia her card. "Please call me if you have a change of heart."

"I'm not giving you or anyone else an interview."

The reporter motioned toward the cameraman that it was time to leave. Julia heaved a sigh of relief when the two left the building. Her heart rate slowly returned to normal. That was a narrow escape.

"Julia?"

Her heart wanted to explode at the pain she heard in Cain's voice as he whispered her name. Whirling around, she found him in the area by the mailboxes, tucked back in the corner close to where the newspapers were delivered. He had the newspaper clenched in his hand. His eyes were wide with incredulity, with disbelief, as if she'd heartlessly thrust a knife into his back.

"You blogged about it? About killing me with kindness?"

Her mouth felt as if it was filled with dry cotton balls. She found it impossible to answer.

"I'm Ebenezer?"

Her eyes drifted closed. Cammie had warned her. This was the worst scenario possible for Cain to learn what she'd done, and now it was being played out before her eyes.

"Answer me," Cain demanded, his disbelief replaced by anger so deep it caused her to flinch.

Julia's eyes flew open. "Yes, you're Ebenezer."

"Why would you do that?"

"I . . . I was asked to do a blog. Two of us were up for the same position working social media for Harvestware. As a final test we were both asked to write a blog. The one with the highest number of followers would be awarded the job."

"The job you got?"

Slowly, she nodded. It wasn't like she could deny it. It hurt to speak and so she swallowed, and answered, unable to make eye contact. "Yes." The word was soft and low, so low she could barely hear it herself.

"You must be thrilled." The comment was weighed down with sarcasm so heavy his voice dropped an entire octave.

Answering him would only condemn her and so she remained silent.

Cain exhaled and leaned his head back to stare up at the ceiling. "I never learn, do I? How could I have been so stupid?"

"Cain, please, let me explain."

His returning laugh was filled with bitterness and anger. "You want to explain? I don't think so. I've heard more than enough already. We're done."

"Please." She placed her hand on his arm, which he quickly shook off as if he found her touch repugnant.

"No. Don't even try. I trusted you the same the way I trusted someone else. With both of you I was simply a means to an end. Nothing more. Someone to be used and discarded once you got what you wanted."

"That's not true. If you'd only listen," she pleaded.

Shaking his head, he walked away and didn't look back.

Julia slumped against the wall, as the weight of all that had happened was more than she could carry or bear. A tingling sensation went through her as she struggled to come to grips with the pain she'd caused him.

Cain was unbelievably hurt, and she was responsible. Knowing what she'd done wounded her, too. When Cain hurt, she hurt. She didn't know if that was what happened when you cared deeply about someone, when you loved them, but she strongly suspected it was.

It went without saying that Cain wouldn't be joining her for Christmas dinner. She assumed he would do whatever possible to avoid being anywhere close to her from this point forward. To him, whatever it was they'd shared was finished. He wanted nothing more to do with her.

Depressed and sick at heart, Julia headed out of the building and started walking. Everyone around her seemed to be in the Christmas spirit, full of cheer and goodwill.

Her, not so much.

She made an effort to smile and return season's greetings, but it demanded more effort than she felt.

An hour later she found herself outside Manor House. She must have walked the three miles, but she barely remembered the long trek. Once Cain's grandfather learned what had happened, he was likely to cancel Christmas dinner with her, too. She wouldn't blame him.

Bernie was in his room, napping in his recliner, when she knocked politely against his door.

"Come in," Bernie called out.

Julia tentatively opened the door and let herself into his small apartment.

He frowned when he saw her and motioned for her to take a seat. "You better tell me what happened," he said, not waiting for her to speak.

"Did you talk to Cain?"

"Briefly."

Julia sat on the edge of the chair and leaned forward, intent to learn everything she could. "What did he say?"

"Nothing much, just that he wouldn't be able to join us for Christmas dinner. Knew right away there was more to it than he was telling me. You want to fill in the blanks?"

She clenched her hands on her lap and looked down at her intertwined fingers. "He found out that I'd been blogging about my kindness project." She glanced up and saw that Bernie was waiting for more of an explanation. "Cain assumed I'd used him to get that job, and the truth is I did. I didn't mean to hurt him, Bernie. I don't think I'll ever forget his expression. It was as if I'd betrayed him the same way that woman he worked with did. I think he hates me." Julia had often heard that the line between love and hate could be paper thin. She believed that now, seeing the look in Cain's eyes.

"What's a blog?" Bernie's frown was intense.

He lowered his recliner and listened intently as Julia explained it to him.

When she finished, she waited impatiently for his reaction. Her fear was that he, like Cain, would condemn her.

"I see what you mean," he said after an awkward moment. "Cain would hate being the focal point of this blog thing."

"I didn't use his name. No one ever needed to know it was him," she said, defending herself, and then hung her head. "It wouldn't take a genius to figure it out, though; I did write that Ebenezer was my neighbor."

"You called him Ebenezer?"

"Yes, when I first started the experiment the name fit, but it doesn't any longer."

"What would you call him now?"

Julia didn't hesitate. "Sweetheart."

Bernie grinned, his eyes brightening with pleasure. "You have feelings for my grandson?"

Julia remembered the disappointment and hurt in Cain's eyes and how it had cut at her, too. "I'm falling in love with him."

Bernie considered her words. "Did you try talking to him?"

"I begged him to give me a chance to explain, but he was having none of it." She could only hope that given time, Cain would be willing to hear her out, although she doubted it would be anytime soon.

At her news, Bernie's shoulders slumped forward and he looked as downtrodden as she felt.

"If he read the blogs himself, then maybe he'd feel differently."

"He won't."

"How . . . how do you know that?" This was her one hope, the only way she would find the path to redemption in Cain's eyes.

"I know my grandson. Cain isn't about to subject himself to any more ridicule than he already feels. The last thing he'll do is read those blogs."

"I didn't ridicule him."

"I'm sure you didn't, but Cain won't see it that way."

The one avenue she had to set matters straight between them was closed. Her gaze reverted to her clenched hands. "He mentioned the other woman . . ."

"Oh yes, you must mean Dani, that girl from work he took an interest in. He never said much about her."

"He claimed we were alike; that he trusted us both . . . basically, that he was a fool for ever having allowed himself to be vulnerable to either one of us." It hurt that Cain would associate her with the other woman. In retrospect, she couldn't blame him. Cain believed she was no better and possibly even worse.

"He's not going to get past this, is he?" she whispered brokenly. Although it was a question, she was well aware of the answer. Covering her face with both hands, she leaned forward and pressed her forehead against her knees.

"Come now, Julia, you can't let my stubborn grandson upset you like this."

She lifted her head as she struggled within herself.

"It's Christmas," Bernie said as he reached out and patted her hand. "These matters have a way of righting themselves. Give Cain time to sort through this. He's a smart boy. Eventually he'll come to his senses."

Julia so badly wanted to believe that was possible. Deep down she knew it could happen, but it wasn't likely. Cain might be a lot of things, but with his background and his experience with women he wouldn't believe Julia was any different. It was almost as if he'd been waiting for her to betray him. It was what he expected, what had been the repeated pattern in his life.

"Will you still come for Christmas dinner?" she asked.

"You sure you want me?"

"Of course I'm sure." She didn't feel much like cooking, but for Bernie she'd make the effort.

"I'll need to rearrange plans with Cain, but that shouldn't be a problem. He doesn't seem to be much in the mood to celebrate. I'll suggest we do brunch." Giving her hand a gentle squeeze, Bernie offered a smile of encouragement. "You go home and do whatever it is you need to do for our dinner and leave Cain to me."

"You're going to talk to him?" It was more than she had hoped.

"No promises, but I'll do my best to get him to listen to reason."

Filled with gratitude, it was all she could do not to leap forward and hug the older man. "Thank you," she whispered.

Hope was intoxicating. Cain loved and respected his grandfather. If Bernie talked to him about the blog, then just maybe he'd give her a chance to make things right. It was the best chance she had of explaining herself, of getting a second chance.

Once she finished her shopping Julia returned to her apartment. Standing in the hallway, her arms loaded down with grocery bags, she paused and stared at Cain's door. In the last twelve days she'd felt like that door had opened to her, inviting her into his life and into his heart. Seeing it now, that same door appeared closed and locked. It made her ache inside to realize all she had lost.

She unpacked her groceries, then she started cooking. The first item on her list was a homemade pumpkin pie. She was up to her elbows in flour when someone pounded against her door so hard it was a wonder his fist didn't go through the wood.

Her blood pressure spiked. It could only be Cain, and from the sound of it he wasn't in the best of moods. It didn't matter. She'd take him any way he chose to reach out to her.

With her apron wrapped around her middle and her hands dusted with flour, she answered the door.

Just as she suspected, Cain stood stiff and proud on the other side. His face was tight and menacing. "Stay. Away. From. My. Grandfather."

She winced at the anger and emotion in him. "Is that what Bernie wants?" She remained outwardly composed, hoping her calm sincerity would have an effect.

"I don't care what Bernie wants. You might have fooled

him but not me. I learned everything I need to know about you this morning."

"You can believe I'm a horrible person, Cain. You even probably think I'm diabolical and selfish and that I used you for my own personal gain. But I would never do anything to hurt your grandfather."

"I don't want you anywhere close to him."

"He's coming to dinner on Christmas."

His eyes narrowed. "Not if I can help it."

They continued to stare at each other, neither willing to back down. Neither willing to give an inch. After what seemed like an eternity, Julia swallowed against the knot in her throat and spoke.

"I'll admit I have my faults, and I'm sure you'd be more than happy to list them for me. It's true I kept the blog a secret. I should have told you. I was wrong to use you as the subject matter without letting you know, I'll readily admit that. But I always believed you to be a fair-minded person. I didn't like you in the beginning, mainly because you were rude to me.

"You can condemn me if that's what you believe, if it makes you feel better about what I did. It might even be what I deserve, but if you do then we're both losers. I've been happier in the last twelve days than I have been in a long while, and I'd like to think you have been, too.

"And here's the thing: I wrote about kindness, wondering if it would make a difference, and when it did, others decided to try it, too. I was shocked with how fast the idea caught on, and the response I got. I truly believe it's done a lot of good and I never meant for it to be at your expense. If you read the blog yourself, you'd see what I mean."

His eyes narrowed to thin slits. "No way am I reading those posts."

His refusal hurt, but she had no choice but to accept his decision. "We had something special, Cain. I'm sorrier than you know that it's over. As for dinner with Bernie, I think it might be best to leave that decision to him."

Julia had said all she could, and when he refused to meet her gaze, she gently closed the door, leaned against it, and released a deep sigh. She swore she could hear Cain on the other side. It felt as if their hearts beat as one. Turning, she pressed her cheek against the door to better hear him. Her hand was splayed against the wood, reaching out to him.

Several minutes passed. Two. Three. Four. Long enough for her to consider opening the door and reaching out to him, not caring if he pushed her away.

Just when she found the courage to reach for the door, she heard Cain move and return to his own apartment.

Julia's Blog

TWELVE DAYS OF CHRISTMAS

December 24

The Final Chapter

Merry Christmas! It's just before midnight on Christmas Eve. I'm back from church and loved hearing the words to my favorite carol, "Mary, Did You Know?" The song asks Mary several questions about this baby she delivered.

It begged the question of me. Did I know when I started this experiment where it would lead me?

I didn't.

I had no clue.

In retrospect, I think my friend who suggested this must have had an idea what would happen. She knows me well. Cammie was sure it would be big, but neither one of us came close to guessing just how big.

This morning I was stopped by a television reporter who wanted an interview. She said this blog has been trending nationwide.

If my words have inspired others, then that inspires me.

My neighbor was unpleasant and unfriendly. I thought—hoped, really—that kindness would change him. It was a challenge even to be in the same elevator with him. He made sure I understood he had no desire for my company, and, frankly, the feelings were mutual. If kindness could change him, then great. Mission accomplished.

The shocking part for me is that kindness changed me, too.

Not only did my attitude toward Ebenezer make a drastic U-turn, but I learned a great deal about myself. I'd allowed his negativity to rub off on me. He didn't like me, and so I made sure he knew I didn't like him, either. That defensive wall went up and I regarded him with condescension. Ebenezer was unworthy of my friendship. As a result, I'd been far too willing to judge him and criticize his behavior.

I've grown a lot in the last twelve days.

As for the question I asked you recently—if I should tell Ebenezer or not—I want to thank you for your responses. It's been an even split—half for and half against.

However, it's a moot point now. He found out on his own and he wants nothing more to do with me. The last thing I'd ever wanted was to hurt Ebenezer, and that's exactly what I've done.

The experiment is over, and while in some ways it might have been a success, I feel like I've failed. I hurt the one person who means the world to me.

Today is the final chapter.

Chapter Twelve

Julia knew spending Christmas Day with Bernie would be a treat and a challenge, seeing that her relationship with his grandson had gone south with the speed of a jet-fueled rocket. He'd changed dinner plans with Cain and the two had gotten together earlier in the day for brunch at Manor House.

"You got your cribbage board ready?" Bernie asked her as soon as he arrived. Standing just inside the apartment door, he closed his eyes and sniffed appreciatively. "It's been far too long since I had a home-cooked Christmas dinner. Smells divine in here."

"I think so, too." Julia had the turkey breast in the oven along with a number of traditional side dishes. It was far more food than the two of them could possibly consume, but she wasn't about to short them. Many of the recipes were family favorites handed down from her mother and grandmother.

The thought of Cain spending the day alone rather than suffer her company pained Julia. The sad part was that there wasn't anything more she could say to change his mind. It would be a waste of breath to try to convince him to join Bernie and her.

As if Bernie could read her thoughts, he came all the way into the apartment, removed his coat and hat, and said, "My grandson is far too stubborn for his own good. At breakfast I asked him to join us. He refused. I tried again just now and got the same response." He set his cane by the sofa and sat down. "That boy is missing out on a mighty fine meal."

Julia didn't mention Cain's visit from the day before when he'd warned her to stay away from his grandfather. She couldn't help but wonder if he'd had the same discussion with Bernie, warning his grandfather away from her. While she was curious, she was afraid to ask, for fear she already knew the answer.

While the turkey breast baked, they played several hands of cribbage and then, sitting side by side on the sofa, watched Julia's favorite Christmas classic movie, *The Bishop's Wife*, with Cary Grant and Loretta Young.

"They don't have actresses like Loretta Young anymore," Bernie commented wistfully. "The stars these days are all wusses. Where are the actors like John Wayne? Now, there was a man."

He didn't really expect an answer, which was a good thing, because Julia didn't have one.

How she wished in their short time together that she could have gone to a movie with Cain. It would've been fun to find a show they could both agree on. Their tastes were vastly different, and finding a compromise would have delighted her. She could almost hear the negotiations and discussions they would need to have.

"What are you thinking?" Bernie asked, studying her closely.

Julia glanced down. Rather than answer, she shook her head to clear her thoughts. "Nothing important."

Bernie didn't buy it for an instant. "It's that stubborn grandson of mine, isn't it? I'll give him a few days to settle down and then I plan to give him a piece of my mind."

"No, don't. Please." The last thing Julia wanted to do was cause problems between Cain and his grandfather. It was difficult enough that Bernie had decided to join her for dinner. Cain was sure to view that as another betrayal and blame her. After Cain's visit she'd tried to talk Bernie out of joining her, but he insisted she not renege.

Bernie's frown betrayed his concern. "I don't know what to do with him."

"Let Cain be. Either he'll work this out on his own or he won't. The choice is his."

Bernie didn't look convinced. "Makes me wonder what I could have done differently when he was a boy. I did the best I could. Heaven knows I loved him but apparently not enough."

Julia leaned over to hug the older man. "None of this is your doing, Bernie. I was the one who used Cain. He has trust issues as it is and I fed into that. This isn't about you; it's between Cain and me."

"If he hasn't got sense enough to realize you're a good woman and he's lucky to have you in his life, then he's an even bigger fool than I thought."

Julia kissed his weathered cheek. "Thank you."

Her words were interrupted by someone at her door. The hard knock told her it had to be Cain. She glanced at Bernie and he winked at her.

Winked.

She paused the movie and then answered the door. Sure enough, Cain stood in the hallway and he wasn't in any better mood than he had been the day before.

"Yes?" she asked.

Cain's eyes went past her to his grandfather. "Despite everything I said, he came, anyway?"

"The decision was his."

"Is that my fool of a grandson?" Bernie called to her from the sofa, although he couldn't avoid seeing that it was Cain. "Of course I came. I didn't pay that taxi to bring me here so you could talk me out of Christmas dinner with a beautiful woman."

Cain clenched and unclenched his fists. "This is your doing?"

Bernie came to his feet, and seeing that he needed his cane, Julia grabbed it and took it over to the older man. He stood on wobbly feet and Julia helped him get upright by supporting his elbow. Bernie tossed her a grateful glance. "Growing old is the pits," he whispered under his breath.

Cain stood stiffly in the hallway, watching Julia aid his grandfather.

"For the love of heaven, come inside," Bernie told Cain. "You want the entire building to hear you making a fuss?"

After a moment's hesitation, Cain came into Julia's apartment and closed the door. "I told you to stay away from Julia," he said, addressing his grandfather.

"Why would I do that?" Bernie leaned both his hands atop his cane.

Cain narrowed his gaze as he looked at Julia. "She's not to be trusted."

Julia did an admirable job of keeping her mouth closed. As it turned out, it wasn't necessary. Bernie took up her defense.

"Julia, untrustworthy?" Bernie laughed as if he found the comment comical. "Because she didn't tell you about the blog. Get over it, boy. Isn't that what you kids say these days? Look at her." He gestured toward her with one hand. "This is a good woman. She brought me cookies, came to visit me."

"The cookies were a bribe."

Julia raised her finger, wanting to remind Cain the cookies were the very ones he'd refused.

Bernie gave a disgruntled huff. "She invited me to Christmas dinner, cooked for two days to make us a traditional meal, one you're a dope to miss, I might add. She didn't need to do any of that. She has friends who invited her to their home and she could have accepted. Instead, she went to all the trouble and hassle of cooking for me."

One look told Julia nothing Bernie said had fazed Cain.

"Furthermore, she's got a good heart. You saw her volunteer to play the piano at Manor House. Took time out of her life to entertain others. And weren't you telling me just the other day how she helped the kids put on a holiday program for the Boys and Girls Club?"

Bernie made her sound like a candidate for sainthood, but he wasn't finished yet.

"There must be something wrong with your head, son." Bernie tapped the side of his own. "Anyone with half a brain should be able to see the kind of woman Julia is. I know she should have told you about that blog thing and from everything she's said, she regrets that and has apologized. You're the one unwilling to forgive."

"Maybe she should write a blog about forgiveness," Cain fired back sarcastically.

Bernie simply shook his head. "I feel sorry for you if you can't get over this, because it's your loss, not hers."

Cain turned his attention to Julia, his gaze holding hers prisoner.

"Now, are you going to stand there like a bump on a log or are you going to come to your senses and apologize?"

"Me apologize?" Cain flared and then coughed out a laugh as if he'd never heard anything more ridiculous. "I don't think so."

Julia stepped forward. "Would it help if I apologized? Again?"

"No." Both Bernie and Cain answered at the same time in the same sharp tone of voice.

Julia flinched. Well, she'd tried.

Bernie swayed on his feet and Julia noticed that he'd

gone pale. "Bernie? Are you feeling all right?" She started toward him, but Cain reached him first and gently led his grandfather back to the sofa and into a sitting position.

"Pills," Bernie murmured, having trouble speaking. "Right-hand pocket."

Julia reached into his coat pocket and retrieved the nitrate pills. She opened the container for him and he placed one under his tongue. Leaning back, he closed his eyes.

"Does this happen often?" she asked Cain.

He looked stricken.

"Should I call nine-one-one?"

Indecision marked his face. "I don't know."

"I'll be all right," Bernie insisted, keeping his eyes closed. "Just give me a couple minutes."

Julia waited, half expecting Cain to blame her for his grandfather's attack. She took Bernie's hand in her own and rubbed it. He seemed to be having trouble breathing. Not knowing what to do, Julia looked to Cain, hoping he'd know what was best.

He seemed to read her mind. "Gramps, to be on the safe side I think we need to have the hospital check you out."

Bernie adamantly shook his head. "I'm not missing out on Christmas dinner with Julia."

"I'll save it for you," she promised.

Cain reached for his phone and made the call.

Julia sat at Bernie's side and continued to rub his hand while Cain raced down to the foyer to meet the paramedics.

Bernie rebounded briefly, but she could see he was in bad shape. It seemed to take an eternity before Cain reappeared with the men from the fire department. The paramedics checked Bernie over and made the decision to transport him to the hospital. While Bernie was loaded onto a gurney, Julia turned off the oven and grabbed her coat and purse.

"Where are you going?" Cain demanded.

That he would ask astonished her. "To the hospital."

His response was a curt nod. "You can ride with me."

For half a second she was convinced she'd heard him wrong and almost asked if he was sure he wanted her company. Smart girl that she was, she responded with a simple "Thank you."

Not a word passed between them on the ride to the hospital. As best as he could, Cain followed the aid car. He was fortunate to find parking on the street and the two of them half walked, half ran toward the hospital's emergency entrance, where the medics delivered Bernie.

As soon as they were inside, Cain approached the reception desk and explained that he was Bernie's grandson and would fill out any necessary paperwork. While Cain dealt with that, Julia found a seat in the waiting room and anxiously awaited news of the older man's condition.

It felt like hours before Cain returned, but it was actually only about fifteen minutes.

"Did they tell you anything?" she asked.

He shook his head. "Not really. The receptionist said she would call my name when the doctor has something definitive to tell me."

The minutes passed so slowly and staring at the wall clock only made it feel slower. Reaching for a six-month-old issue of *Good Housekeeping* magazine, she flipped through the pages but was unable to focus. Setting it aside, she bounced her hands against her knees until Cain reached over and blocked the movement. It would have helped if they could talk, but as it was, Julia had to hold all her worries inside.

"He's a tough old bird," Cain said after several more tense minutes. "He'll be fine."

Now that he'd broken the ice, she felt free to continue the conversation. "Has he had these episodes in the past?"

Cain nodded. "A couple times. His heart is weak, which is why I moved him into Manor House. I can't be with him all the time and this way the staff can keep an eye on him."

They were quiet again and another sluggish fifteen minutes passed.

Julia released a long, slow sigh. "I'm worried, Cain."

To her shock, he reached over and took her hand, holding it tightly between his own. The small act of comfort and reassurance nearly brought tears to her eyes. She swallowed against the building lump in her throat and she curved her fingers around his, holding on to him the way a kitten clings to the high tree branch.

They sat in silence for several more minutes. When Cain spoke, his voice was low and controlled. "I read your blog."

Julia was stunned and froze, waiting for him to say something more. He didn't. When she felt like she could speak, she asked, "Do you hate me more now?"

Frowning, he turned to stare at her. "I could never hate you, Julia."

He said that now, but just the day before he'd looked at her with contempt when he'd learned what she'd done.

"Thank you for that."

His hand tightened on hers. "You were right. I did find you irritating in the beginning."

"I was trying too hard," she whispered, thinking her morning chatter those first few days had been over-the-top.

"Perhaps I wasn't trying hard enough."

She couldn't believe that he was sitting with her and holding her hand and talking to her.

"That last post, you wrote that kindness changed you."

"Yes."

He sighed. "It changed me, too."

"Cain Maddox." A male nurse appeared and called out his name.

Both Cain and Julia bounded to their feet as if they'd been shot out of a rocket and approached the man.

"I can take you back to see your"—he hesitated and looked down at the clipboard—"your grandfather."

"Thank you."

The nurse looked to Julia. "Are you a relative?"

Before she could answer, Cain said, "She's with me."

The nurse nodded and then led them both to the cubicle where Bernie lay on the bed. The first thing Julia noticed was that his color was better. The doctor appeared a few minutes later.

"We'd like to run a few tests, which will mean keeping him overnight."

"No way," Bernie protested. "Not on Christmas. Julia's cooking and—"

"No arguing," Cain chastised him.

"Don't worry, Bernie, I'll save dinner for you."

"I'm not letting you spend Christmas alone," Bernie objected.

Cain bristled. "Would you stop worrying about Julia? She's fine. You're the one with the heart condition."

"Don't fight it, Bernie," Julia advised. "You've got two nurses, a doctor, and your grandson against you and I'm joining forces with them. Best to do what they advise."

"But—"

"Bernie, please."

The older man sighed and then reluctantly nodded at Julia. "Only because you asked."

Cain's face tightened. "I see you've got him wrapped around your little finger, too."

Too? The implication being that she had control of him as well.

The doctor exited the cubicle, giving the nurse instructions, which left Bernie with only Cain and Julia. Cain's grandfather studied the two of them.

"You talking?" he asked.

Julia waited for Cain to answer, and when he didn't she did. "A little." Then, lowering her voice, she added, "He read the blog."

"I'm right here," Cain returned stiffly. "There's no need to whisper."

Bernie rolled his head against the pillow and focused his

attention on Cain. "You read it?" he asked, as if he found it hard to believe.

Cain folded his arms over his chest and nodded. "Is there a problem with that? Were they password-protected?"

"Of course not," Julia assured him. "The reason he's asking is because he told me you wouldn't." Because she was afraid he might misunderstand her, she added, "I'm grateful you did."

"Well, well," Bernie said, grinning from ear to ear. "Guess my grandson's still got it in him to surprise me."

"Wipe that look off your face, old man. I still don't trust Julia; nor should I."

Bernie snorted and likely would have said more if not for the fact that the nurse returned. "Time to take you to your room, Mr. Maddox." He glanced toward Cain and Julia. "If you'll return to the waiting area, I'll get your grandfather settled. Once I do, I'll let you know his room number."

"Thank you," Julia whispered.

Doing as instructed, they returned to the waiting room and reclaimed the very chairs they had vacated only a few minutes earlier.

Once seated, Julia kept her gaze focused straight ahead. "I'm grateful you let me go with you to see him."

Cain shrugged as if to say it wasn't a big deal. "If I'd gone back there alone, Bernie would probably have kicked me out and asked for you."

Picturing Bernie doing exactly that, Julia smiled. "Too?" she asked.

"Too what?"

"You said I had Bernie wrapped around my little finger, *too*."

"Slip of the tongue. You might have had me at one time, but not now."

"Oh." She did her best to hide her disappointment. All at once everything was too much for her. If Cain had read her posts and was still unwilling to forgive her, there was nothing left for her to say. Afraid she was about to do something that would embarrass them both, she left the waiting area. Not knowing where to go or what to do, she walked down the hallway and paused, wrapping her arms around her middle, and looked out of the window onto the landscape outside.

To her surprise, after a few minutes Cain followed and came to stand behind her, his hands on her shoulders. Their gazes met in the reflection in the window.

He rested his chin on the crown of her head and exhaled a deep sigh. "I want to be more than the means to an end to you."

"You already are, Cain, so much more than you realize."

His hands tightened on her shoulders.

"Don't you know how important you are to me, or how I feel about you?" Risking her heart and her pride, Julia turned and wrapped her arms around his middle, pressed the side of her face against his chest. "Didn't my blogs tell you how hard I was falling for you?"

"No," he admitted. "All I saw or felt was how quickly you managed to worm your way around my heart. I told you once I didn't like the way you made me feel. You were becoming a necessity, and that shook me."

"I remember." She held that conversation vividly in her mind because his words could easily have been her own.

"I lied," he whispered, kissing the side of her face. "I cherished every minute we shared. Everything felt fresh and new and alive when I was with you. I hadn't felt that way in years. It intoxicated me. You intoxicate me."

Julia broke away enough to look up at him, hardly able to believe what she was hearing. Her heart swelled at his words and she bit into her lower lip, fighting back emotion.

"I had a hard time believing this was real," he continued. "I was convinced that sooner or later I'd learn this was all a hoax, so when I heard that reporter talking to you, it was as if I'd known all along that something like this was bound to happen. It was what I'd expected, what I'd come to anticipate."

"Oh, Cain, don't you know? Don't you see?" She placed her palm against his cheek, cupping the side of his face. As she looked into his eyes, she hoped he could read all that she was feeling.

He took hold of her wrist and moved her hand toward his mouth so he could kiss the inside of her palm. "I am so wrapped up in you that I doubt I'll ever be the same again."

Julia smiled, her heart so full it felt as if it was about to burst. She would have said more, but the nurse came looking for them.

"Your grandfather is in his room now, if you'd like to see him."

"Please," Julia answered.

Once given the room number and the directions, Cain

took her hand once more. Happy as she was, Julia felt like skipping.

Once inside the elevator, Cain worked his arm around her shoulders. "I should have held out longer, let you think the worst."

"Cain."

"I'm a stronger man than this."

"Really?" She knew it was his pride talking and didn't take offense.

"You made me weak."

"Is that a good thing or is it bad?"

"Depends. In this instance I'd say it's to be expected, seeing how you have completely won me over."

"What you don't seem to understand, Cain Maddox, is that I'm equally under your spell. Everything you've said is happening to me, too. I've been an emotional mess ever since that reporter showed. I couldn't bear the thought of hurting you, because when you hurt I hurt."

The elevator doors opened and they made their way down the corridor until they found Bernie's room number. He looked to be sleeping when they entered, but he must have heard them because he opened his eyes. For a long moment he stared at them as if he wasn't sure he recognized who they were. Then a huge grin spread across his face.

"I see you two have settled matters."

"We did," Julia said, her arms wrapped around Cain's waist and his around hers. Cain looked down on her, his eyes warm and loving.

"Good thing," Bernie murmured.

"It's a very good thing," Julia agreed.

"Then get busy, you two. I'd like to live long enough to hold a great grandchild or two."

"Gramps, hold up, you're moving way too fast," Cain warned.

"I'm not getting any younger, you know. Get a move on."

Cain grinned and looked at Julia. "You gonna blog about this, too?"

"Absolutely."

He chuckled, and turning her in his arms, he kissed her as if she was his last meal, and she returned his kiss as if he was hers.

Julia's Blog

TWELVE DAYS OF CHRISTMAS

December 25

Christmas Wishes Coming True

Merry Christmas! Again. I actually thought yesterday was the end of the experiment. But I was wrong.

There is an epilogue to my story.

It all started with Ebenezer's grandfather and ended with me in Ebenezer's arms.

Yes, my friends, I'm in love.

Impossible, you say. No one falls in love in twelve days. But we did. I mentioned just yesterday how being kind changed me. Unexpectedly, it opened up my heart to the very person I thought was a grouch. Kindness showed me there was far more to this man than meets the eye.

It opened up Ebenezer's heart, too. He saw me as an annoyance, but after only a few days his opinion changed.

If kindness can alter two people's attitudes toward each

other, just imagine what it could do to change our world, one relationship at a time.

I want to thank you, too, for your encouragement and support through this journey. I've appreciated your comments and suggestions. I've learned a lot from you and taken your advice to heart.

I'm going to continue with my blog and with the kindness project.

Ebenezer has said he'd like to join me; we're going to work together.

So once again, my friends, Merry Christmas.

"God bless us every one."

And yes, I'm quoting Tiny Tim, but still, it seems rather fitting, don't you think?

One Year Later

CHRISTMAS

Bernie sat in the living room of Julia and Cain's small house, sniffing appreciatively toward the kitchen. Julia had just finished basting the turkey while Cain put the finishing touches on the table setting. Schroeder and the Irish setter puppy Cain got Julia for Christmas were snuggled up against Bernie's feet. A puppy Julia had christened Blossom.

She'd been working her dream job at Harvestware for almost a year now. She loved every minute and was able to telecommute three days a week, which made getting the puppy possible. She'd married Cain in June after a whirlwind courtship. Everything had fallen into place like easy-fitting puzzle pieces after she'd started the kindness experiment. She'd fallen in love with Cain, met Bernie, was hired for her dream job, and married Cain, and just a month ago they'd purchased their first home with a fenced yard for the puppy.

Cain stepped up behind her and wound his arms around her waist and nuzzled her neck. "Merry Christmas, Mrs. Maddox."

Julia turned and looped her arms around his neck. "Back at you, Mr. Maddox." As long as she lived, she would never tire of the comfort of being in her husband's arms.

"You two getting all lovey-dovey on me again?" Bernie called out from the other room. He sat in front of the television, sorting through a stack of holiday movies, choosing the one they would watch while their dinner finished cooking. "I still don't have any news about that great-grandchild. In my day me and your grandmother got right down to business. What's the holdup with you two?"

"Gramps, we've barely been married six months. Give us time."

"You get a puppy but want to wait on a baby?" Bernie shook his head. "You sure you know what you're doing, boy?"

Julia laughed. "He knows, Bernie, trust me, he knows. Give us at least a year, okay?"

Cain's grandfather relaxed against the sofa back. "I suppose I can wait that long. Now are we gonna watch a Christmas movie like we started to last year?"

"Which one did you choose?" Cain asked.

Bernie handed him the DVD.

"*The Bishop's Wife?*" Cain groaned. "Again?"

"You love that movie as much as I do," Julia reminded him.

"What I love is having you cuddle up against me and seeing how happy it makes you."

Julia smiled up at her husband, her eyes full of promise. "I know how to make you happy, too, you know."

He grinned. "I do, and it doesn't have anything to do with movies."

The doorbell rang in short, impatient bursts.

Cain cast a questioning glance at Julia, who shrugged. She had no idea who it could be.

Breaking away from her, Cain answered the front door. Julia recognized the woman who stood on the other side as their next-door neighbor. They'd met only once briefly, and she hadn't seemed overly friendly.

"Mrs. Quincy, is everything all right?" Cain asked. "Do you need anything?"

"I most certainly do," she said with a huff. "A section of my fence is down and I want to know what you did."

"I did?" Cain asked, clearly taken back by the question.

"Well, I didn't knock it over, so it must have been you."

"I can assure you I didn't."

"Don't care if you did or not, you need to fix it." With that she gave a snort and stomped away.

"Well, that old biddy," Bernie flared as Cain closed the door. "She's got her nerve."

Frankly, Julia agreed, and then reconsidered her attitude. "I wonder if Mrs. Quincy has any family," she said.

Cain turned to face her, his look stern. "Julia?"

"Yes, love," she replied innocently.

"I know that look," he muttered.

"What look?" Bernie demanded. "What are you two talking about?"

"Mrs. Quincy," Cain explained.

"That woman who looks like she's been sucking lemons half her life?" Bernie asked. "The one who came to your front door just now?"

"The very one," Julia said, catching Cain's eye. "Seems to me she could use a little kindness."

A slow grin came over Cain. "You might be right about that."

Bernie slapped the sofa, tilted back his head, and rolled his eyes. "Oh, for the love of heaven, not again."

"Not to worry," Julia said, wrapping her arms around her husband's waist. "I have no intention of blogging about it."

"Don't be hasty," Cain said, grinning.

"Why don't we invite Mrs. Quincy over for Christmas dinner?" Julia suggested. "That would be a good place to start, wouldn't it?"

"It would."

Cain kissed the tip of her nose, grabbed his jacket, and hurried toward the front door after Mrs. Quincy.

Blossom started after Cain, and Julia captured her Christmas puppy just before she flew out the door. Standing in the doorway, she watched her husband approach the older woman and saw the look of surprise that came over the older woman's face.

Mrs. Quincy hesitated and then nodded.

Yes, this was going to be an extra-special Christmas with a puppy, a surly neighbor, and an extra dash of love.

If *Twelve Days of Christmas* warmed your heart,
you won't want to miss Debbie Macomber's
next delightful Christmas tale

Merry and Bright

Continue reading for a special sneak peek.
Available now from Ballantine Books.

Chapter One

MERRY

"Mom, I need to work overtime, so I won't be home to help with dinner."

"Again?" her mother moaned into the phone.

"Yes, sorry." Merry hated leaving her mother with the task of cooking dinner. Robin Knight struggled with mobility issues due to complications with MS. As much as Merry hated the thought of it, her mother would soon be confined to a wheelchair.

"That's three nights this week."

Merry didn't need the reminder. Three nights out of four. Matterson Consulting, the firm where she worked as a temp, was involved in a huge project, its biggest one to date, for the Boeing Corporation. With the time crunch, everyone on staff was putting in mandatory overtime. Normally, few would object to the extra hours, but this was the holiday season. People were busy, and there were parties to attend and shopping and decorating that needed to be done. Baking. Visiting. All the normal, fun things that were part of this time of year. For those employed by Matterson, it didn't matter. Christmas might as well be blocked off the calendar.

"Don't worry, dear," Merry's mother assured her gently. "Patrick will help me with dinner."

Merry closed her eyes and let her shoulders sag. Patrick was a dear boy, but he tended to dirty every dish in the house when he cooked. Her eighteen-year-old Down syndrome brother was the light of her life, but his help in the kitchen was questionable at best.

"Heat up soup and have Patrick make sandwiches," Merry suggested.

"We can do that, but you should know Bogie is out of dog food."

Bogie was Patrick's golden retriever and had an appetite that rivaled that of an entire high school football squad. Grocery shopping was a task Merry had taken on as her mother's illness progressed. However, working the hours she did made it nearly impossible to find the time needed. "Oh Mom, I'm sorry. Poor Bogie. I'll stop off at the store on my way home and pick some up." While she was there she'd grab a few other essentials, too, like milk and bread. They were running low on both. And maybe some ice cream for Patrick, who never complained about the need to help his mother.

"Your father can do that on his way home—"

"Don't ask Dad," Merry interrupted. Her father was a

pharmaceutical salesman and traveled extensively around the Pacific Northwest and was often on the road. He carried a heavy enough load as it was. By the time he got home from driving across the state, he'd be exhausted. Merry didn't want to burden him with any extra chores. He did enough as it was. Buying the groceries was her responsibility.

Everyone worked together in the Knight family. They were a tight-knit group by necessity and by love. Merry had taken the twelve-month temp job with Matterson Consulting to save tuition money for college. Her educational expenses were more than their family budget could manage. She'd been hired by Matterson Consulting specifically for this Boeing project and had worked extensively on inputting the data. It'd taken months to accumulate all the necessary information. It was all winding down now. December 23 would be her last day on the job.

After working with the company for nearly a year, she'd made friends with the other two women working in data processing. They considered her part of the team and often turned to her with questions, as she had replaced the department head. Although she was only a temporary employee, her skill level was above those currently assigned to the project.

Merry took another bite of the peanut-butter sandwich she'd brought for lunch. She usually ate at her desk and worked through her lunch break. Most everyone else went to a local café around the corner, where the food was fast, cheap, and tasty. All three were necessary if Merry was going to splurge and eat out. She treated herself once a week, but more often than that would play havoc with her budget. Most days she brown-bagged it and ate at her desk.

"When was the last time you went out, Merry?" her mother asked.

"I go out every day," she answered, sidestepping the question.

"On a date."

"Mom! When do I have time to date?" Merry had a fairly good idea what had prompted the question. Her best friend from high school had recently announced she was pregnant.

"That's exactly my point. You're twenty-four years old and you're living the life of a nun."

"Mom!"

"Patrick dates more than you do."

Merry had to smile even though her mother was right. Her younger brother was involved with a special group that held dances and other events that allowed him to socialize with other teens who had Down syndrome. As a high school senior, he was active in drama and part of the football team. He had a girlfriend as well.

"It's time you stopped worrying about your family and had some fun."

"I have fun," Merry countered. She had friends, and while she didn't see them often, they were in touch via social media, email, and texting. If Merry was busy, which she tended to be, then she communicated with emojis. It was fun to see how much she could say with a simple symbol or two.

"Have you ever thought about joining one of those on-line matchmaking sites?" her mother asked, sounding thoughtful.

"No," Merry returned emphatically, rolling her eyes. She hoped the state of her social life would change once she could afford to return to school. It wasn't like she was a martyr, but at times she struggled with the weight of family obligations. She tried not to think about everything she was missing that her friends enjoyed. It was what it was, and it didn't do any good to feel sorry for herself. Her family needed her.

"Why don't you try it? It'd be fun."

"Mom, have you seen all the forms and questionnaires that need to be filled out for those dating sites? I don't have time for that." *Especially now, with the demands of my job,* she thought to herself.

"Make time."

"I will someday," she said, hoping that would appease her mother.

"*Someday,* Merry? Failing to plan is planning to fail."

"Mom. You sound like Anthony Robbins." Although she complained, her mother was right. The timing, how-ever, was all wrong.

"I'll think about it after the first of the year," she promised.

Her best friend Dakota had met the love of her life on Mix&Mingle.com. Inspired by Dakota's success, Merry had checked out the site but had gotten bogged down with the page upon page of questions that needed to be completed. She started filling out the forms but quickly gave up, exasperated by all the busywork.

"You need to get out more, enjoy life," her mother continued. "There's more to life than work and more work."

"I agree. After the holidays. Let me finish this temp job first."

"It worked for Dakota."

"Mom, please. I have plenty of time to get out there." Merry didn't need the reminder about her friend's happy ending. After Dakota met Michael on the site, she had sung the website's praises to Merry like a wolf howling at the moon. She wouldn't stop bugging Merry about it until she'd promised to give it a try.

"I heard from her mother this morning. Did you know Dakota and Michael are expecting?"

"Yes, Mom, I heard." Merry reached for her sandwich and was about to take another bite when the vice president of the company, Jayson Bright, walked past her desk. He had to be one of the most serious-minded men Merry had ever met. To the best of her memory she had never seen the man smile. Not once. He looked about as happy as someone scheduled for a root canal.

Jayson Bright paused and stared at Merry. His eyes fell to the name plate on her desk. MARY KNIGHT. She'd asked HR to correct the spelling of her first name twice, with no success, and then gave up. Seeing that she was a temp, they hadn't shown that much interest. Her boss's gaze landed on the sandwich she had on her desk, and for a moment she toyed with the idea of offering him half, but as she doubted he'd find any humor in it, she restrained herself. He arched his brows before he walked away.

"Merry, did you hear me?" her mother asked.

"Sorry, no, I was distracted." From Mr. Bright's look, Merry had to wonder if there was something written in the employee handbook about eating at one's desk. She'd been doing it for almost a full year now, and no one had mentioned that it was frowned upon before.

"Merry?"

"Mom. I need to get off the phone. I'll call you before I leave the office."

"Okay, but think about what I said, all right?"

"Okay." Merry's mind filled with visions of meeting her own Prince Charming. Of one thing she was certain: It wouldn't be someone as dour as Jayson Bright.

Sure enough, just as Merry suspected, at three that same afternoon, a notice was sent around the office.

It is preferred that all staff refrain from eating at their desks. For those who choose to remain in the office for lunch, there is a designated room provided. Thank you.

Jayson Bright
Vice President
Matterson Consulting

Merry read the email and instinctively knew that this edict was directed at her. She preferred to avoid the lunchroom, and with good reason. The space was often crowded and it was uncomfortable bumbling around, scooting between those at the tables and those waiting in line for a turn at the microwave. Besides, it was more efficient to eat at her desk. Not that Mr. Bright seemed to notice or care.

What a shame—the company vice president was such a curmudgeon. Merry had heard women in the office claim he was hot. She agreed. Jayson Bright was hot, all right. Hotheaded! He was young for his position as vice president. The rumor mill in the office said he was related to the Matterson family; the company president was his uncle. Bright would assume the role when it came time for his uncle to retire. His uncle would continue as chairman of the board.

Merry's thoughts drifted to Jayson Bright and she mused at how attractive he would be if he smiled. He was about six feet tall, several inches taller than her five-five, with dark brown hair and eyes. He kept his hair cut in a crisp professional style. Wanting to be generous in spirit, Merry supposed he carried a heavy responsibility. Word was that Jayson Bright was the one responsible for obtaining this Boeing contract. A lot weighed in the balance for him with his job. Merry knew that he put in as many hours, or more, than the rest of the staff.

By the time Merry arrived at home, hauling a ten-pound bag of Bogie's favorite dog food, it was after eight o'clock. As soon as she walked in the door, Patrick rushed to help her with the heavy sack.

His sweet, boyish face was bright with enthusiasm.

"Merry's home," he shouted, taking the dog food out of her hands and carting it to the kitchen pantry.

"Hi, sweetheart," her mother called. Her mom leaned heavily on her walker, now exhausted and fatigued, because she grew tired at the end of each day.

"Can I tell her?" Patrick asked excitedly.

"In a minute," her mother said. Merry noticed that her lips quirked with the effort to hold in a smile.

"Tell me what?"

"We got you an early birthday gift this afternoon and it's the best one ever." Patrick rubbed his hands together, unable to disguise his eagerness.

"You did?" Knowing the family budget was tight, Merry wasn't expecting much. Born on December 26, the day after Christmas, Merry had felt cheated as a child when it came to her birthday gifts. Her parents had done their best to make her birthday special, but its being so soon after Christmas made that difficult. It wasn't unusual for Merry to get her birthday gifts early because of it.

"And you're going to be so happy," Patrick assured her. "I helped Mom with everything."

"You helped pick it out?" Merry asked. The two of them must have ordered something off the Internet, because her mother was no longer able to drive and Patrick couldn't. Those with Down syndrome could legally drive in Washington State, but the family couldn't afford a second car. The family had only the one car, which her father used for work. Merry used public transportation to and from her job.

"Well, this isn't something we picked out. You need to do the picking."

"Patrick," his mother chastised. "You're going to give it away."

"You can show me after you feed Bogie," Merry suggested, as Bogie eyed the bag of dog food.

"We can't really give it to you yet," Patrick told her. "You get to pick for yourself, but I'll help if you want." From the way his eyes lit up, Merry knew he'd be terribly disappointed if he didn't get a say in this.

Okay, now Merry was willing to admit she was intrigued. It was still November, a week after Thanksgiving. Her brother was barely able to contain himself and rushed to grab Bogie's food dish. She enjoyed his enthusiasm. Seeing the happy anticipation in him piqued her own. She couldn't imagine what this special birthday gift could possibly be.

Bogie pranced around in his eagerness for Patrick to fill the dish so he could eat.

"Now, Mom, now?" Patrick asked, jumping up and down after he poured the dog food into the bowl. Between the dog and her brother, the two looked like they were doing a square dance.

"Let me eat dinner first," Merry said, teasing her brother.

Patrick's eyes rounded. "Merry, no, please. I've been waiting and waiting to tell you. I don't think I can wait any longer." Merry and her mother shared a smile.

"Have pity on the boy," her mother urged.

Holding back a smile would have been impossible. "Okay, Patrick, you can tell me about my birthday gift."

Her brother's eyes lit up like Fourth of July sparklers. Whatever this early birthday present was must be special. Merry hugged her brother and, wrapping her arms around his torso, she gave him a gentle squeeze.

Patrick took hold of her hand while their mother opened the laptop and pulled out a chair to sit down. Merry joined her mother.

"You ready?" Robin Knight asked, turning on the computer.

"I can hardly wait," Merry answered.

Tucking his arm around her elbow, Patrick scooted close to Merry.

She looked at the blank computer screen, getting more curious by the second. They both seemed to be squirming with anticipation. "What did you two order me?"

Patrick laughed and pointed to the computer, crying out, "We got you a *man* for your birthday!"

"What?" Merry asked, certain there was some misunderstanding. "I don't think it's possible to buy me a man."

"Not exactly buy," her mother explained. "Patrick and I spent the afternoon answering the questionnaire for Mix&Mingle.com. We filled in your profile and signed you up for the next six months."

Merry was speechless for several moments. *"You did what?"*

"We got you a date," Patrick answered, beaming her a huge smile.

If she wasn't already sitting, Merry would have needed

to take a seat. Her immediate thought was how best not to disappoint her mother and brother by telling them this wasn't anything she wanted. That thought was quickly followed by a question. "What photo did you use?" She hoped it was a recent one and not some high school prom picture. She'd changed a lot since her teen years. She wore contacts now instead of glasses, which showed off her deep brown eyes; her hair was longer now, shoulder length, parted in the middle. She'd be mortified if they'd used the photo on her employee badge for Matterson Consulting, where she looked like a deer caught in the headlights. Actually, it resembled more of a mug shot.

"That's the best part," Patrick told her, looking well pleased with himself. "We didn't use a photo of you."

Now Merry was totally baffled. "You mean to say you posted a picture of someone else?"

"Don't be silly," her mother responded.

"Well, if it isn't me, then whose photo did you use?"

Patrick's glee couldn't be contained. "We used Bogie's."

"You made me a dog?" Merry cried, resisting the urge to cover her face. "Why?"

"Two reasons," her mother explained.

"One," Patrick intervened, thrusting his index finger into the air, ready to show his reasoning. "You love dogs."

"Ah . . . I guess," Merry admitted. Bogie was as much her dog as Patrick's. He often slept on her bed. She took him for walks on the days Patrick couldn't. Bogie was considered part of the Knight family.

"And second, and most important," her mother continued, "you're a beautiful young woman. Too many potential dates would judge you purely on your looks. That didn't sit right with me. I wanted them to get to know you as a person, as the generous, kindhearted, loving woman you are. They will need to dig deeper into your profile rather than to simply gaze at a photograph. And," she added, "we weren't sure how you'd feel about all of this, so we chose a pseudonym for your name. You are now Merry Smith."

"Merry Smith," she repeated slowly, still having trouble taking all this in. Looking at her profile as it came up on the screen, she withheld a groan. Seeing Bogie with her pseudonym listed below, she figured it was highly unlikely anyone would send her a Mix&Mingle message. Anyone looking at the photo would think her profile was all one big joke. No one wanted to date a dog.

Join DEBBIE MACOMBER
on social media!

Facebook.com/debbiemacomberworld

Twitter: @debbiemacomber

Instagram: @debbiemacomber

Pinterest.com/macomberbooks

Visit DebbieMacomber.com
and sign up for Debbie's e-newsletter!